Welcome to Springwater, Montana . . .

In full command of the storytelling magic that has made her a beloved, best-selling author, Linda Lael Miller spins her triumphant Western novel *Springwater* into a charming new series.

SPRINGWATER SEASONS is a breathtaking slice-of-life in a frontier town that's growing from little more than a whistle-stop into a bustling Montana community. You will never forget the men and women who fall in love in these splendid tales, and you'll thrill along with them as Springwater blossoms with friendship, love, and laughter.

Don't miss a moment of life in Springwater—be sure to read these magnificent novels, each one a thrilling piece in the patchwork quilt that is

Springwater Seasons

RACHEL
January 1999

SAVANNAH
February 1999

MIRANDA
March 1999

JESSICA
April 1999

Praise for

My Outlaw

"Ms. Miller's time travel novels are always precious but this one surpasses them all. The premise is incredibly invigorating, the passion hot and spicy. Memorable characters link it all together to create a keeper."

—*Rendezvous*

"Miller's reasoning is brilliant and will fascinate time-travel aficionados. . . . This sexy, smart, heart-stirring love story fulfills romance readers' dreams. This is destined to be a favorite."

—*Romantic Times*

"In one thousand years, a panel of twentieth-century experts discussing time travel novels will first talk about the works of H. G. Wells and Linda Lael Miller. [This] time travel romance has everything a reader could want in a novel. The story line is exciting and action-packed, with an incredible heroine who will do anything to save her beloved's life. *My Outlaw* is a keeper that will stand the test of time. . . . FIVE STARS."

—*Affaire de Coeur*

"Exhilarating. . . . Linda Lael Miller still reigns supreme in the time travel romance universe."

—Amazon.com

Books by Linda Lael Miller

Banner O'Brien
Corbin's Fancy
Memory's Embrace
My Darling Melissa
Angelfire
Desire and Destiny
Fletcher's Woman
Lauralee
Moonfire
Wanton Angel
Willow
Princess Annie
The Legacy
Taming Charlotte
Yankee Wife
Daniel's Bride
Lily and the Major
Emma and the Outlaw
Caroline and the Raider
Pirates
Knights
My Outlaw
The Vow
Two Brothers
Springwater

Springwater Seasons
Rachel

Linda Lael Miller

SPRINGWATER SEASONS

Rachel

SONNET BOOKS

New York   London   Toronto   Sydney   Tokyo   Singapore

This book is a work of fiction. Names, characters, places and incidents are products of the author's imagination or are used fictitiously. Any resemblance to actual events or locales or persons, living or dead, is entirely coincidental.

An *Original* Publication of POCKET BOOKS

A Sonnet Book published by
POCKET BOOKS, a division of Simon & Schuster Inc.
1230 Avenue of the Americas, New York, NY 10020

ISBN: 0-671-02684-4

First Sonnet Books printing January 1999

10 9 8 7 6 5 4 3 2 1

SONNET BOOKS and colophon are trademarks of Simon & Schuster Inc.

Front cover illustration by Robert Hunt

Printed in the U.S.A.

June of 1998
Port Orchard

Dear Friends,

Welcome to the Springwater stagecoach station, which will grow over the next few months, before your very eyes, into a thriving community, complete with a saloon, a schoolhouse, a church, and a newspaper, among other things. There are six books in the Springwater series, although I may do more. I love the idea of writing a long, involved story and watching this fictional town full of delightful people come to life. I hope the many and varied characters will become as dear to you as they are to me.

Let me know what you think, and to receive a copy of the *Springwater Gazette,* Springwater's own newspaper, please send a business-sized stamped, self-addressed envelope, with your address clearly printed. We'll add you to the newsletter list automatically, thus giving you advance notice of every new release, whether it is part of this series or not. The address is:

Linda Lael Miller
P.O. Box 669
Port Orchard, WA 98366
e-mail: lindalaelm@aol.com

God bless and keep.

Warmly,

Linda Lael Miller

For Amy Pierpont,
with love and appreciation

❧ Spring ❧

**Near Springwater,
Montana Territory, 1874**

CHAPTER

1

TREY HARGREAVES HAD BUSINESS to attend to that chill and misty day in early spring; he was dressed for courting and in a fair-to-middling hurry, so he very nearly rode right on by when he spotted the stagecoach bogged down square in the middle of Willow Creek. The driver, a strapping, ginger-haired young Irishman by the name of Guffy O'Hagan, was fighting the mules for all he was worth, but the critters had gotten the better of him and there was no denying it.

It wasn't that the creek was exactly dangerous, Trey thought, reluctantly drawing the black and white paint gelding to a halt on the bank to survey the scene proper-like. The water was fast-moving, what with the thaw and all, but it was no more than four feet deep, and a person would have to be downright stupid to drown in a trickle like that.

He sighed. The problem was, there were a surprising number of stupid people, even in these isolated parts, out beating the brush for a chance to get themselves killed. While he had no real worries about Guffy, the man being no sort of greenhorn, he wasn't so sure about the woman. First of all, she was wearing a blue feather on her hat, a bedraggled, plumelike thing, bent at one end—by the ceiling of the stage, no doubt—and second, she was halfway out the window, fluttering a handkerchief at him like some duchess summoning a servant.

He sighed again.

Her voice rang out over the rush of the stream, the infernal splashing and the bellows of the balking mules, not to mention Guffy's loud litany of forbidden Anglo-Saxon words. Clearly, he'd forgotten that his passenger, traveling alone as far as Trey could tell, was a lady.

"Sir!" she cried, with more waving of the handkerchief. "Pardon me, Sir? Are you an outlaw?"

Trey allowed himself a semblance of a smile; perhaps the woman was more perceptive than he'd first thought. Did they show, all those years when he'd been a wanderer and a scoundrel, making his living mostly by gambling and serving as a hired gun?

He ignored her question, sighed once more, and sent the paint wading into the icy water. His pant legs were soaked through by the time he reached the door of the marooned stagecoach, and his boots were full. He'd be lucky if he didn't lose a couple of toes to frostbite.

Close up, he could see that the stranded lady was young, barely out of her girlhood, probably, and more than passingly pretty. Her hair was auburn, a billow beneath that silly feathered hat, and her eyes were someplace between gray and green. She had good skin, long lashes, and a soft, full mouth that made Trey ponder on what it would be like to kiss her.

"As you can see," she said primly, in starched Eastern tones, "we are in need of assistance. First, though, I should like you to answer my question. Are you an outlaw, Sir?"

Trey wanted to laugh, but he didn't. He was afraid she'd stop being funny, out of sheer cussedness, if he gave in to the urge. "Well, Ma'am," he said, "I reckon that depends on who you ask." He touched the brim of his hat when he saw the flicker of alarm in her eyes. "Name's Trey Hargreaves and, for the most part, I've contrived to stay on the right side of the law. I reside at Springwater," he cocked a thumb over one shoulder, "back that way a few miles."

At the mention of Springwater—he didn't flatter himself that his name had wrought the change—her eyes lit up and some color came to her cheeks. "Thank heaven," she said. "It has seemed to me that we would never arrive. Especially since we've run aground here in the middle of this . . . this river." She nodded to indicate the roof of the coach, where a great deal of baggage was affixed with rope. "If we should overturn, the books would be lost, and I don't need to tell you, if you come from Springwater, what a dire event that would be. Without education, the children will be left to the influences of places like the"——she lowered her voice confidentially here, and lent the words a dire note——"like the *Brimstone Saloon*."

It was all Trey could do, and then some, not to laugh out loud when she said that. As it was, he felt the corners of his mouth twitching dangerously, but he managed to retain a somewhat sober expression. "God save us all," he said, with fervor, and laid one hand to his breast.

Her eyes narrowed for a moment; she was bright, that was clear enough, and she'd discerned that he was pulling her leg a little. She put her hand out to him. "My name is Rachel English," she said. "I've been engaged to teach at the new school in Springwater."

The coach swayed dangerously, nearly turning onto its side, and Miss English drew back the hand she'd offered to hold her hat in place. With the other, she clutched the window's edge, and the expression of thwarted fear in her face tugged at Trey, in the empty place where he'd once kept his heart.

"I can wade ashore," she said. "I can even swim a little, if need be. But those textbooks mustn't be ruined. Please, Mr. . . . Mr. Hargreaves, lend us your assistance."

"Sit tight," Trey counseled her. Then he reined the paint toward the front, where the mules were still carrying on fit to whip up a froth on the water. "How-do, Guffy," he greeted the youthful driver, with a grin and a tug at the brim of his hat.

"Not real well," Guffy ground out, cordial enough,

considering he had both hands full of reins and fractious jackass. "If you'd kindly . . . get the lady on solid ground . . . I'd have less . . . on my mind."

Trey made another motion, as if tipping his hat, and rode back to the door. Bending down, he turned the latch and pulled—no easy task, even with his strength, with the rushing water working against him.

"Come on," he said to Miss English, and curved one arm to reel her in.

She drew back, and it struck him that she could probably show those stage mules a thing or two about digging in their heels. "The books—" she said.

Trey was wet and he was cold and he was hopelessly late. He was not, therefore, of a mind to argue. "I'll get the damnable books," he said. "But only when you're out of this coach and standing on the bank over there."

She grabbed a small, tattered handbag and something that looked like a plant cutting from the seat beside her. "Very well," she said, "but I will hold you to your word, Sir."

Trey hooked an arm around her waist—she was hardly bigger than a schoolgirl and weighed about the same as a bag of horse feed—and hauled her, her unwieldy plant stem, tiny handbag, and all, up in front of him, just this side of the saddle horn. She smelled of roses after a rainfall, Trey thought, in a fanciful fashion that was utterly unlike him. She might have just climbed out of a bathtub and dried herself off, instead of traveling three-quarters of the

way across the country. If she was the new schoolmarm, she was Evangeline Wainwright's friend, sent
for from Pennsylvania, and the topic of such interest
around Springwater that even he had heard of her.
From his daughter most especially; Emma eagerly
anticipated her arrival.

Holding her fast, lest she slip away and float
downstream like so much flotsam, Trey squired the
new teacher to the Springwater side and set her on
her feet. She clutched her bag, the plant cutting
wrapped at the roots in damp cheesecloth, and her
dignity, and there was a plea in her eyes as she looked
up at him.

"The books, Mr. Hargreaves," she said.

"Trey," he replied, sounding foolish even to himself. He turned the paint away and the two of them
splashed quickly back to the coach.

"I could use some weight up top," Guffy said,
breathless from the battle. "You mind climbin' up,
Trey? Go round the other side, so you don't tip the
damn thing over."

Any fool could have seen what needed doing, but
Trey overlooked the unnecessary specifics of the suggestion, given the state of Guffy's nerves, and made
his way to the far side of the coach. There, grasping
the framing of the baggage rack, he raised himself to
stand in the saddle, then scrambled upward. The
stage swayed perilously for several moments while Trey
spread his weight as best he could, like a high-wire
artist seeking balance.

The rig finally settled, though, and the animals

calmed down a little. The paint plodded his way back to the shore and up the bank, reins dragging, and shook himself off like a dog, thereby baptizing Miss Rachel English in the ways of the wild and wooly West.

"Come on down here and take the lines," Guffy shouted back, over one meaty shoulder. "I'm going to see if I can persuade that knucklehead out there in the lead to point himself in the right direction."

Trey nodded and made his way carefully to the box, where he took up the reins, watching as Guffy climbed nimbly over one mule's back and then another, until he was mounted on the animal in front, on the left.

"Mr. Hargreaves!" he heard a voice call. "Oh, Mr. Hargreaves!"

Exasperated, Trey turned his head and saw the schoolmarm with her hands cupped around her mouth. He was too annoyed, and too busy with the reins, to reply.

"Don't forget about the books!" she called, and pointed with one hand to indicate the roof of the coach.

He heaved yet another sigh and ignored her. She was as exasperating a female as he had ever come across, and he felt sorry for the man who would eventually marry her. Someone surely would though, trial that she plainly was, for women were scarce in those parts, especially passably pretty ones, like her.

Suddenly, miraculously, the wheels of the coach grabbed and lurched forward, and the eight mules pulled as one, rather than in all directions, as they had before, nearly pitching a distracted Trey into the water. At a careful pace, the stage gained the bank and lumbered, dripping, up over the muddy slope, onto the grass.

The mules stood shuddering, wet through to bare hide, and looking even more pathetic than mules commonly do.

Miss English picked her way toward the sodden coach, stepping daintily over mud and stones and slippery grass. The feather on her hat looked somewhat the worse for wear, but it still bobbled foolishly in the breeze. Trey couldn't help noticing her womanly shape as she approached, though; perhaps because of the hectic nature of their encounter, he'd somehow overlooked that particular aspect of her person, despite the fact that he'd practically carried her from the stage to the shore just a few minutes back.

"I suppose I should thank you for your assistance, Mr. Hargreaves," she said, with restraint, clutching her plant cutting in both hands. "Alas, you did not heed my instructions concerning the crate of books."

He secured the reins and climbed down from the box to execute a sweeping bow and open the door of the coach. Only the most extreme forbearance kept him from telling her what to do with her books. "I seldom heed instructions, Ma'am," he said, "unless, of course, they're called for, which yours were not."

She blushed and clambered into the dripping rig, fussing with her skirts in a hopeless effort to keep the floor from wetting her hem. Guffy, meanwhile, had gotten back to the box and taken the reins in hand.

"I see you have no appreciation for the value of an education," she said.

Trey suppressed a grin. "On the contrary, Ma'am," he countered good-naturedly, but with a sting, "I hold the skills of reading and ciphering very dear. If that coach had turned onto its side, though, I reckon most everything would have been lost—the rig itself, the freight, and half the mules. You might not have fared too well either, and Guffy, well, he could have gotten himself crushed without even trying. So good day to you," he made to tug at his hat brim, but the hat was gone, probably a mile downstream by then, "and think nothing of it. You're mighty welcome."

She flushed all over again at that, and a pretty sight it was, too. Almost fetching enough to make Trey forget that he'd never make it over to Choteau, some twenty-five miles away, in time to stop Miss Marjorie Manspreet from getting onboard an eastbound stage and leaving his life forever. He'd gotten a late start as it was—maybe he *had* dallied a bit, back at Springwater, though he had a whole string of excuses at the ready—and now it was downright hopeless. He'd have to ride the rest of the day and much of the night to get there before Marjorie lit out, and he just didn't feel up to making the effort.

He whistled to the paint, which ambled toward

him in obedient response, while Miss English put her head out the stage window. "I apologize," she said briskly. "You were quite helpful, and I should have thanked you."

"Not at all," he said, and that time he did grin. There was just something about her that drew that response from him. He turned his attention to Guffy, who was beaming down on him from the box, the spring sun shining around his big frame like an aura.

"Much obliged, Trey," he said.

Trey mounted the paint and leaned down to gather the reins in his hands. "Come by if you're staying over. We'll discuss the trials and tribulations of skinning mules."

Guffy laughed and nodded, setting the team in motion again, making for Springwater, and the stagecoach station that had given the place its name. Another team would be waiting there, and maybe even a relief driver, if the gods were smiling. With luck, the boy might get himself a night's sleep in a clean bed, some of June-bug McCaffrey's legendary cooking, and a few well-earned shots of whiskey down at the Brimstone—on the house, of course.

Since Emma, Trey's eleven-year-old daughter, was visiting the Wainwright ranch for a while, in order to help with the housework and the little boy and keep her good friend Abigail company, Miss Evangeline being exceeding pregnant these days, he decided to follow the stage in, dry off a little, and take a meal at the station himself. If there was any justice at all in the world, Miss June-bug would have made up a batch of her baking soda biscuits to go with supper. Trey had a powerful yearning for biscuits and besides, he'd lost a perfectly good hat and a prospective wife helping Guffy get the coach across the creek. He deserved *something* as a reward, and the taste of Miss June-bug's cooking would serve for now.

Rachel was sick unto death of that dratted paeonia cutting, which she had nursemaided all the way across country, forever taking care that it wasn't crushed, that it didn't dry out, that it wasn't left behind on some sooty train seat or in some rustic station along the way. She probably would have flung the thing out the stagecoach window long since if it hadn't been for Evangeline's wanting it so. Dear Evangeline, her good and trusted friend. She could hardly wait to see her again, to look into her eyes and find out if the happiness glowing in her letters was shining there, as well.

No one on the face of the earth, Rachel firmly believed, was more deserving of marital bliss than Evangeline Keating Wainwright. Not that Rachel was even remotely interested in marriage on a personal level. No, there had been but one man for her, Langdon Pannell, and he had died in the war, so horribly, so senselessly. She could not and would not take the risk of loving so thoroughly again; her grief over Mr. Pannell had shaken the very depths of her spirit. Besides, in a rash and reckless moment, she had given herself to him, the night before he rode away to fight, and he had given himself in return. Their communion had been so complete, a fusing of souls really, that for Rachel, even the prospect of lying with another man seemed a travesty.

She was thinking these thoughts as the stagecoach rolled and jostled over the last few muddy miles to Springwater, where the stream called Willow Creek had its beginning, according to Evangeline's letters. She was honest enough to admit that she was watching their erstwhile rescuer, riding along beside the coach, while she reflected. He was a handsome man, in a rakish sort of way, with dark hair tied back at the nape of his neck, and eyes the color of mercury. She hadn't been able to help noticing his eyes; she'd never seen any quite like them.

There was a scar, long healed, along the edge of his jaw, and he was big; to Rachel, who was diminutive, he seemed almost as large as the horse he rode. The man and his mount gave the impression, in fact, of a war monument come to life, all brick and bronze and stubborn majesty.

She sat back and closed her eyes, but the image of Trey Hargreaves and his warhorse stayed with her. That set a vague sense of panic astir in her, for in those moments, Langdon was but a shadow in her memory, without face or feature. She sat rigidly upright, and fixed her eyes on the opposite wall of the coach, upon which someone had posted a tattered bill that read, "Repent or burn. Thus sayeth the Lord."

"Thus sayeth you," Rachel grumbled, and ripped

the bill down. She'd been looking at it ever since she'd
left the last coach, at Choteau, and boarded this one.
She crumpled the warning and tossed it onto the
floor. Dear heaven, but she was weary of traveling—
she longed for a hot, savory meal, a night of sound
sleep, and the near-forgotten pleasure of getting about
on her own two feet. Rachel was a great walker, and
she had sorely missed that pastime over the weeks
she'd spent in transit.

At last, she heard the driver, Mr. O'Hagan, hail
someone from his perch in the box of the rig, and the
vehicle itself sprang violently from side to side as he
hauled back on the reins, shouting to the mules, and
set the brake lever. "Springwater station!" he called
out, with a jubilant note in his voice.

Rachel slid across the hard, narrow seat of the
coach and peered out at the station house. It stood on
the far side of what looked like a full acre of mud, and
someone had laid down rough-hewn boards as a sort of
walkway. A beaming woman in a calico dress and an
apron stood on the step, waving, while a large man of
somber countenance made his way along the zig and
zag path of planks. Here, of course, were the McCaffreys, the town's founders and leading citizens. It had
been Jacob and June-bug McCaffrey who had seen
that the schoolhouse got built, according to Evangeline, and they'd rounded up the funds to send for her
and a supply of primers as well.

"Hello, Miss English," Mr. McCaffrey said, in his
impossibly deep voice, opening the coach door and
putting out a work-worn hand. "Welcome to Spring-

water, such as it is. We were beginning to fret about you."

"We run into some trouble at the creek," Guffy put in, before Rachel could reply. "Hadn't been for Trey here, we'd still have trout swimmin' betwixt our spokes."

Jacob concentrated on helping Rachel down before acknowledging Hargreaves with a noncommittal nod of his head. "Obliged," he said.

"Don't mention it," Trey replied, his tone as clipped as Jacob's. "You have another driver here? Old Guffy's had a hard day. I promised him some consolation whiskey."

It seemed to Rachel that Jacob bristled beside her; not surprising, she thought. After all, Evangeline had told her a great deal about the McCaffreys in her letters, for she considered them dear friends. Jacob was a preaching man, as well as the stationmaster, and therefore liable to take a dim view of whiskey drinking. As Rachel did herself.

In the end, though, Jacob simply shrugged and said, "You look a mite used-up yourself, Trey. You're welcome to stay for supper if you'd like."

Trey grinned full out, a devilish, boy's grin, and Rachel was dumbstruck by the change it wrought in his face. "Nobody but a fool would turn down one of Miss June-bug's suppers," he said.

Miss June-bug was waiting on the porch, her eyes shining. The woman was close to sixty, Rachel knew, but there was a glow about her that made her seem twenty years younger. "We're mighty glad you've come to us," she said, and embraced Rachel warmly.

It brought tears to Rachel's eyes, that simple human contact. She did not think anyone had embraced her since Evangeline and Abigail had set out, four long years before, on their splendid adventure.

"The girl is plumb tuckered," Jacob observed. "You look after her, Miss June-bug, and I'll spoon up some of your chicken and dumplin's for Guffy and Trey."

"You bring a plate for Miss English first," June-bug said, taking Rachel by the arm and leading her over the threshold and into the fragrant warmth of the station. There were long tables set throughout the room, six in total, and a blaze crackled merrily on the hearth of a great stone fireplace. "Guffy and Trey will manage just fine on their own."

With that, Mrs. McCaffrey squired Rachel to a room at the very back of the station. It was a small chamber, with a high window, and the bed looked inviting, plain though it was. Just an iron frame, two pillows, and an old, faded quilt. Nearby was a table, with a freshly filled kerosene lantern and a box of matches close at hand. There were pegs on the walls for Rachel's clothing and a pitcher and bowl of plain red and white enamel stood on a rickety washstand in the corner.

"We can heat up some water for a bath once you've eaten, if you'd like that," June-bug said quietly.

Like it? Rachel's eyes stung with tears of joy and relief at the mere idea. It would be her salvation, after all those days and nights spent traveling, first on various trains and then on stagecoaches. She had managed only furtive washings along the way, and she needed a bath as much, if not more, than she needed sleep and food.

"You're very kind," she murmured, with an accepting nod. "Thank you."

Mrs. McCaffrey cast an eye over the paeonia cutting. "I could put that in water for you, too. Looks like it's lost most of its starch."

Rachel smiled at the idiom and handed over the cutting. "Evangeline asked me to bring it," she said, "and I don't mind admitting that I've grown tired of babying the thing. No doubt I'll forget what a trial it was, when I see the first blossoms."

June-bug looked at the start with such longing then that Rachel found herself wishing she'd brought two, difficulties be damned. "That will be a sight to see," the older woman said, on a long breath.

"The blooms are this big," Rachel replied, making a plate-sized shape in the air with both hands. "I'm sure Evangeline will be happy to give you a cutting, once the plant's established."

June-bug beamed. "I reckon you're right," she said. "I'll be sure to ask her soon as I get the chance." With that, the stationmistress left Rachel to look at her accommodations—she would be boarding with the McCaffreys for the foreseeable future—and the other woman had just left when Guffy knocked at the still-open door, bearing the satchel and small trunk that held her personal belongings.

"Ma'am," he said, eyes averted, and blushed as deeply as if he'd found her naked in that room, instead of just sitting on the edge of the bed, trying to gather her wits.

"Thank you," she said, and meant it.

No sooner had Guffy gone than Jacob appeared, carrying a wooden tray filled with food. He brought a bowl of chicken and dumplings, steaming and fresh, and a cup of coffee besides. In addition, there was bread and a weathered-looking apple.

Rachel moved the lamp and matchbox to the washstand, and Jacob put the tray down on the bedside table. It made her feel a bit guilty, being waited on, as though she were playing the invalid to avoid having to do for herself. A farmer's daughter, the youngest and only girl in a family of four, Rachel was not unaccustomed to work.

"I could have eaten at the table," she protested gently.

Jacob treated her to one of his rare smiles; Evangeline had described him very well in her letters, so well that Rachel felt as though she already knew him and Mrs. McCaffrey. Odd, she thought, that there had been no mention of Trey Hargreaves, either for or against. On the other hand, Evangeline was no gossip, for all that she professed to enjoy a generous serving of scandal with her tea—that was one of her finest qualities, her willingness to believe the best of people until they proved her wrong. Rachel wished she herself were half so charitable.

"You've had a long trip," Jacob said to her. "You

take your rest while you can get it. You won't have too many pupils at first—only a dozen or so, from the ranches and farms near enough for the children to make the trip—but you'll have your hands full all the same."

Rachel wanted to ask about Mr. Hargreaves, who he was, where he'd gotten that scar on his jaw, and a hundred other things, but she knew her curiosity wasn't suitable, so she quelled it. She could and would ply Evangeline for whatever details might be forthcoming.

Having served her meal and offered his plain counsel, Jacob left the small room, closing the door behind him. Rachel devoured the delicious food—June-bug's reputation as a cook was wholly justified—and continued to assess the room as she did so. Having been a schoolteacher since she was sixteen, nearly ten years now, she reflected with disbelief, Rachel had boarded with all sorts of families. As humble as this chamber was, she'd never lived in a better one—the log walls were thick, and there was an inside shutter for the glass window. The mattress felt as though it were stuffed with feathers, instead of straw, and the floor was made of solid planks, planed smooth and set tightly in place, so the draft wouldn't seep between the cracks. There were no visible mouse-holes and no spider webs. Furthermore, the bedding smelled of spring sunshine and laundry soap, and she ventured to hope that the sheets were fresh.

Even on the few nights when the stagecoach had

stopped for a night, she'd slept sitting up in the dining room, for it was common practice in hotels and way stations for several guests of the same gender to share a bed, with no allowances made for matters of hygiene or term of acquaintance. Privacy was, of course, impossible in such circumstances, and in any case Rachel was not willing to close her eyes in the presence of a stranger. She was, as a consequence, utterly exhausted.

She ate as much of the food as she could, then carried the tray out to the kitchen area herself. June-bug was already heating bathwater in a number of kettles, and she smiled, pleased that Rachel had eaten well.

"You go on in there now and put your feet up. Jacob will tote in the tub in a minute, and then I'll carry the water. It's nice and hot."

Again, Rachel's gratitude was such that she could barely keep from embracing the woman and slobbering all over her with wails and sniffles. "Thank you," she said, with hard-won dignity. She was a grown woman, after all, and should have been past such wild swings of emotion, whether she was tired or not.

An hour later, she was climbing out of her bath, scrubbed clean and smelling of the rose-scented soap she'd bought before leaving Pennsylvania. Rachel was a great believer in the restorative powers of perfumed soap; hadn't Evangeline mentioned, more than once, how much the cake she'd given her as a farewell gift had meant to her, out there on that isolated ranch?

After drying off with a towel from the wooden rod above the washstand, Rachel took a nightgown from her satchel and shook it out. The garment was chilled, and slightly damp, from the creek crossing, no doubt, but it was a great improvement over the clothes she'd worn for the better part of a week. She got into bed, stretched, and tumbled into a fathomless sleep, never stirring, even when Trey and Jacob came in to carry out her tub.

CHAPTER

2

THE SCHOOLHOUSE, hardly more than a glorified chicken coop, might have been a profound disappointment to Rachel if she'd had any choice but to dig in and make the best of the situation. It measured no more than twelve by twelve feet, that little structure, and the floors were bare dirt. The stove was roughly the size of a milk bucket and could not be counted upon to heat even so small a space as that one in the midst of a Montana winter, nor did it seem particularly safe. There were no desks, only three short rows of benches, hewn from logs and still splintery at the edges. Birds were nesting in the rafters, and there was just one window, behind the crudely made table that was to serve as her desk, and in any case it was dirty enough to filter out any available daylight.

For all its shortcomings, Rachel realized, the Springwater school represented a concerted effort on the part of the locals. Clearly, folks had scrounged and salvaged what they could, and valuable time had been taken from ranch and farm work in order to put up the building.

Grateful that the school term would not begin until the last part of August, Rachel set herself to preparing, sorting the primers brought from Pennsylvania—the pages were only slightly warped from the dampening at Willow Creek—sweeping the floor and routing an assortment of critters, planning lessons for pupils at various levels of education. She composed letters to certain charitable organizations back East, prevailing upon them for slates, maps, a chalkboard, and other necessary items.

All this took a week, and then Rachel found herself in unfamiliar straits: She had nothing to do. June-bug would not allow her to help with the cooking and spring cleaning at the station, and although she was most anxious to be reunited with Evangeline, the Wainwright ranch was a good distance away. Certainly too far to walk and, according to Jacob, too dangerous a trip for an unaccompanied woman.

At first, Rachel spent a great deal of time standing in the bare-dirt dooryard of the schoolhouse, looking across the road at the Brimstone Saloon and fuming at the injustice of it all. The place was not at all what one would expect of a frontier establishment of that nature, neither ramshackle nor rustic, and certainly not weathered. In point of fact, it was downright fancy—whitewashed, with a row of trimmed windows across the second floor. There was grass growing out front, and every day the portly bartender came out, persnickety as an English butler, and picked up any empty bottles and cheroot stubs that might be lying about. It galled Rachel not a little that such an institution should thrive, while the school, the very future of the town and the territory, went begging. It had galled her even more to learn, on her second day in Springwater, that Trey Hargreaves, the man who'd rescued her and the town's schoolbooks, owned half interest. Furthermore, there were regular brawls at the Brimstone Saloon, and the place drew every reprobate who chanced to be passing by. Not to mention attracting drovers and, with them, their herds of bawling, dust-raising, long-horned cattle.

Fretting, of course, was a fruitless enterprise, and so in time Rachel decided to ignore Mr. Hargreaves *and* his business enterprise entirely. She got a list of the six families who would be sending their children to the school come fall, borrowed a retired coach horse from Jacob, and set out to visit each home.

The Bellweathers, Tom and Sue, lived at the edge of a clearing, some two miles from the schoolhouse, in a well-kept cabin. Their ten-year-old daughter, Kathleen, was a lively, spirited child, plain as the proverbial mud-fence and totally unconcerned by the fact. Rachel liked her straight away.

Tom was a lean and wiry man, with friendly eyes and coarse black hair that hinted at Indian heritage, while Mrs. Bellweather, Sue, was timid, with a look of bleak bewilderment lurking behind her shaky smile. "I don't see where Kathleen needs fancy schoolin'," she said, seeing Rachel off at the end of the visit. "She can read some—Tom taught her from the Good

Book—and all she's likely to do is get married and have young'uns anyhow."

Rachel had faced this philosophy before, in the East, and it never failed to rankle. Long experience had taught her, however, to look past this ill-founded belief, for there were nearly always deeper reasons for such prejudices. She suspected that, in this instance as in many others, there had been other children in the family once, some older than Kathleen, very possibly, and gone from home, and some younger, and no longer living. The loss of one child, let alone several, usually made a woman more protective of those remaining. No doubt Mrs. Bellweather was simply afraid to let her daughter make the two-mile trek to and from school each day, and Rachel could sympathize.

Standing beside the borrowed horse, reins in hand, she assessed this earnest and careworn woman with gentleness and respect. "It's important for Kathleen to learn as much as she can," Rachel said cautiously. "And to be with other children. Perhaps Mr. Bellweather wouldn't mind riding with her in the mornings, at least part of the way, and coming to meet her in the afternoons."

"There's no time for such as that," Mrs. Bellweather scoffed, though mildly. Something—irritation, perhaps—flashed in her eyes, and was quickly quelled. "We're plain folks, Miss English. We work from sunup to sundown just to keep body and soul together. We need Kathleen right here."

Rachel held her ground. "I've no doubt that Kathleen is a great help to you. Perhaps, though, for her sake, you'll find a way to spare her, just during the school term. I promise you, Mrs. Bellweather, that your daughter will have a better life if she attends class regularly for the next few years."

"Tom's set on it," Mrs. Bellweather confessed, with a long sigh. Then she gestured to a little grove of trees, birches and cottonwoods mostly, some distance from the house. Squinting, Rachel saw what she had half-expected to see—grave markers, tilting wooden crosses set into the ground. "We had two little boys, once," Kathleen's mother went on. "They died right after we settled here, of a fever. There was three little girls, too, all of them come after our girl, Kathleen. One of them wandered off one day, her name was Betsey, and got herself drowned in the pond back there in the woods. Little Anna, she fell underfoot when Tom was workin' with some horses and was trampled afore he could get to her. Then there was Mary Beth. The fever got her, like it did her brothers." The woman paused, let out a shuddering breath. "Kathleen's all we got left to us."

Rachel wanted nothing so much as to put her arms around the other woman and weep with her, weep because life could be so hard, so brutally hard. She'd learned for herself, though, that the shedding of tears was a waste, and besides that, Mrs. Bellweather had little enough besides her dignity. She wasn't likely to welcome a display of pity. "While she's with me," Rachel said, "I'll take care of her."

"I reckon that has to be good enough, the way Tom

feels on the matter," Mrs. Bellweather answered, resigned. "But I'm still agin the whole idea. I don't mind tellin' you that much."

There wasn't a lot Rachel could say in response to that; she thanked Sue Bellweather for the tea and hospitality, said she looked forward to seeing Kathleen at school on the last Monday in August, and mounted Jacob's old horse to ride off.

By then, it was mid-morning, and Rachel, having breakfasted early with June-bug and Jacob, was hungry. She waited until she was out of sight of the Bellweather place before ferreting through her saddlebags for the fried egg sandwich she'd made before leaving the station. She consumed half of it in a few distracted bites, put the rest away, and rode on, musing over the directions Jacob had given her when she set out.

She would visit the Kildare place, a small ranch owned by a widower, who had, according to the list June-bug had made out, two sons, Jamie, eight, and Marcus Aurelius, age ten. She was still smiling over Marcus's lofty name as she guided the horse up a steep sidehill and into the woods. A good part of her mind remained with little Kathleen Bellweather and the burdens being the only surviving child had placed on her. Due to these distractions, she was upon the makeshift camp before she even suspected that it was there.

A fire burned in a circle of stones, and there was a wheelless Conestoga wagon, with a rough lean-to woven of branches beside it. Rachel was just about to call out, announcing her presence and apologizing for the intrusion, if the inhabitants proved unfriendly, when a small, freckled face peered around the back end of the wagon.

"Who are you?" the child demanded. A boy, Rachel saw, nine or ten at most, with straight fair hair that continually fell into his eyes, bare feet, and rags for clothing.

"My name is Rachel English," Rachel answered, climbing down from the horse and feeling the corresponding sting in the balls of her feet. She walked most places, and though she was a competent rider, she was not used to the saddle. "What's yours?"

"You'd better git before my pa comes back," the boy warned.

Rachel looked around at the small, forlorn camp, which showed little or no sign of an adult presence. There seemed to be no food, and there was no livestock, either. "Tell me your name, and then we'll talk about your father," she said, making no move to mount up and ride away.

"Toby," the boy spat. "Toby Houghton. You happy now?"

Rachel merely smiled, for she saw through Toby's bravado. He was small, he was hungry, he was alone, and he was afraid.

"My pa's gonna be back any day now," Toby insisted. "Any minute, mostly likely."

Rachel nodded sagely. "I see. How long has he been away?"

Toby dragged fine white teeth over his lower lip

while he considered his reply; his blue eyes were sharp
and slightly narrowed as he studied Rachel. She added
intelligence to her assessment. "A long while, I
reckon," he admitted, at great length. "But he's
comin' back. I know he is."

"When was the last time you had something to eat,
Toby?" Rachel asked, careful to keep the pity she
couldn't help feeling out of her voice and her expression.

"I shot me a squirrel just yesterday," he said. He was
as grubby an urchin as Rachel had ever laid eyes on,
and she felt a deep and immediate connection with
him. They had something in common, the two of
them—they were both essentially alone in the world,
strong people set on making a place for themselves.
His father had abandoned him, and his mother was
probably dead. Rachel's family had been splintered—
her three brothers permanently divided by the war and
scattered all over the world by then, her parents long
since gone on to whatever reward awaited them, worn
out by their struggles to keep a struggling farm in the
black.

Rachel turned and raised the flap on her saddlebags, taking out the other half of her sandwich, still
wrapped in one of June-bug's cloth napkins, and
offered it in silence.

Toby withstood the temptation as long as he could,
but in the end pride gave way to hunger, and he darted
forward, snatched the food out of her hand, and
gobbled it down with a desperation that would have

brought tears to Rachel's eyes, if she'd allowed them leave.

"I think you'd better come to town with me," she said, when the brief frenzy was over and Toby was fit to listen. "Just until your pa gets back, I mean." God knew where she would put the child—she could hardly promise the McCaffreys' hospitality, without even consulting them—but she couldn't just leave him there, either.

Perhaps he might find a place at the Wainwright ranch with Scully and Evangeline and earn his keep helping out with the chores, she thought. If Evangeline had said it once, she'd said it a hundred times, and always with that special, joyous exuberance Scully had brought to her life—there was no end to the work on that place. Spring, summer, winter and fall, day and night, there was always something needing to be done.

Toby looked eager, but at the same time, troubled. "What if my pa don't know where I got off to?" he worried aloud.

"He'll know," Rachel said evenly. He'd know a few other things as well, this irresponsible, vanished man, when she got through pinning back his ears for him. "Get your clothes, Toby. We're going to town."

He hesitated, then went back to the dilapidated wagon, crawled inside, and came out again a few minutes later with a small bundle. He waited, gentleman-fashion, until Rachel was mounted, then put his foot in the stirrup and clasped her hand so she could pull him up behind her. His skinny arms rested gingerly around her waist.

"My pa's gonna be real mad," he warned.

"Don't worry about your pa," Rachel replied. "I'll deal with him when the time comes."

Half an hour later, they were at Springwater, approaching the station. To Rachel's consternation, Mr. Hargreaves was there, one shoulder braced against the frame of the open door, a match stick between his teeth. Guffy O'Hagan was sitting on the step, ready and waiting for the next stage to come in. When it arrived, he would help Jacob exchange the team of horses or mules for a fresh one, then take over for the other driver.

"Who do we have here?" Jacob asked, with one of his slow grins, coming around the corner of the station and seeing Toby slide to the ground, clutching his bundled belongings. Jacob's sleeves were pushed up and his clothes were dirty; it was plain that he'd been working in the stables out back. The stage line owned some forty horses, and caring for them required a lot of hard effort.

The boy stood stiffly, his head tilted way back so he could look Jacob in the face. Toby introduced himself.

"Well, howdy," Jacob said, shaking the lad's hand. His eyes met Rachel's, questioning. "Why don't you go on inside and tell my wife—her name's Miss Junebug—that I said to feed you as much as you can hold?"

Toby took to the offer and went inside, casting

tentative, cautious glances at Trey and Guffy as he passed them. It was almost as if he expected one of them to reach out and grab him, drag him back, send him packing. Most of his life, Rachel suspected with a pang, Toby Houghton had been unwelcome wherever he went.

"Where did you find that poor little mite?" Jacob inquired of Rachel, his voice quiet. His rugged, timeworn face was full of compassion and some old and private grief.

"He was alone in a little camp, not far from the Bellweather place," Rachel said. She was still standing beside the horse, reins in hand, and when Trey came toward her and Jacob, her heartbeat picked up speed, a development that pleased her not at all.

"That would be Mike Houghton's boy," Trey said. "There's never been a man more useless than Mike is."

"That's so," Jacob agreed, in his taciturn way. It was a damning statement, coming from him, for in the short time Rachel had known the McCaffreys, she'd learned that they were warmhearted people, inclined to think well of their neighbors, even when they didn't approve of their actions. Trey Hargreaves, with his half-interest in the Brimstone Saloon, was a prime example. They spoke highly of him, and evidently made him welcome whenever he chose to come calling.

"Toby swears his father will be back for him," Rachel said, but with little conviction. Even as she uttered the words, she knew it wasn't going to happen, at least, not anytime soon. Houghton had forsaken his son, simply left him to fend for himself, in a wilderness that had been the breaking of many a full grown man, and strong ones, at that.

"I reckon Miss June-bug would like a lad to feed and fuss over," Jacob mused, gazing toward the house now, with a faraway expression in his deep brown eyes. "She's missed our own boys something fierce. We both have."

Rachel knew a little about Will and Wesley McCaffrey, both of whom had fallen at Chattanooga, again because Evangeline had written her about them. Like most of the other soldiers, on both sides of the conflict, they had been far too young to go off to the fighting, leaving families and sweethearts and unfinished lives behind them.

Rachel was saved from replying by the distant sound of an approaching stagecoach, driver shouting and cursing, harness fittings jingling, hooves pounding on hard-packed ground. Guffy bolted eagerly to his feet and Trey caught hold of Rachel's arm and pulled her out of harm's way, the elderly horse naturally following.

"Best to stand aside," Trey said.

Rachel met his eyes squarely. "No doubt you know Toby's father quite well. He would be the sort to frequent a saloon, wouldn't he?"

A small muscle flexed and unflexed in Trey's jaw, just above the long scar. "That was unworthy, Miss English," he said tautly. "My saloon is a place of business, not a den of iniquity, and I'll thank you to remember that."

"Nothing good can come of whiskey drinking and carousing, Mr. Hargreaves," Rachel responded, in chilly tones, but she'd lost some of her sense of conviction. As far as she knew, there was no gambling at the Brimstone Saloon, and certainly no trading in flesh. On the other hand, with a name like that place had, it was probably only a matter of time before sin and depravation broke out on every front.

Hargreaves leaned in closer and spoke in a hoarse whisper. "I hope you won't let your blue-nosed, back-East disapproval of me spill over onto my daughter, Miss English, because if you do, you and I will have words. Loud ones."

Rachel stared at him, amazed. "You have a daughter?"

He smiled. "I'm quite capable of making babies," he said. He paused, plainly enjoying Rachel's reaction to that forthright statement. "Her name is Emma, she's just about to turn twelve, and right now she's staying with the Wainwrights. She'll be back any day, though, soon as the baby is born and the missus is up and around again, I suppose, and she'll want to meet you. She's been real excited ever since she learned you were coming to Springwater, Emma has, and I *do hope*, Teacher, that you will not disappoint her."

Rachel was flabbergasted, and not a little troubled by the knowledge that if Trey Hargreaves had a daughter, he probably had a wife, too. She didn't want him to have a wife, though she couldn't have explained why, even to herself. "Mrs. Hargreaves?" she inquired, in what she hoped was an ordinary tone. "Where is she?"

"Dead," Trey answered flatly. His face had gone hard all of the sudden, and he turned without another word and walked away, toward the Brimstone Saloon, leaving Rachel to stare mutely after him.

In the meantime, the stagecoach had arrived, disgorging a flock of hungry passers-through, and Miss June-bug was busy inside the station, serving fried chicken, mashed potatoes, gravy, and corn fritters. Toby sat at one end of the table nearest the cook-stove, eating with both hands, while the passengers scattered themselves about the room, probably as glad of a few solitary minutes as they were of a hot, nourishing meal. As Rachel well knew, the inside of a coach could be a cramped and most uncomfortable place, where some loquacious travelers had been known to hold forth on every sort of subject for mile after mile.

"You be wanting that old horse again today?" Jacob asked, at her elbow, coming over the threshold with hat in hand. He gave a half smile, seeing Toby tucking into his food.

"I suppose it's too late to get to the Kildares' and back before sundown," Rachel mused.

"That it is," Jacob agreed. "Best save that errand for tomorrow, unless you're a hand with a shootin' iron." His expression didn't change, but the light in his eyes might have been mirth; it had the sunny effect of a broad, mischievous grin.

Rachel laughed. "I ride well enough," she answered, "but I don't shoot. I'll stay right here and try to persuade Miss June-bug to let me help her with the washing up."

"She might just give in," Jacob speculated, watching his wife bustle happily between the tables with a large blue-enamel coffeepot in hand. "Knowin' her, she's probably already worked out where to get some clothes for that boy and how to wrassle him into a bathtub. That'll occupy her for the better part of the night, I reckon."

"Is there a place to buy clothing?" Rachel asked, puzzled. As far as she knew, there wasn't a store in miles.

"My June-bug is a wonder with a needle and thread, and every time the peddler comes through, she buys a bolt of cloth. Time that boy gets up in the morning, she'll have made him trousers and a shirt, sort of like them elves in that fairy tale about the shoemaker."

Rachel was touched. "She's a wonderful woman," she said.

Jacob's gaze was tender as he looked upon his wife. "None better," he agreed.

Rachel thought to herself that if she could be loved like that, and love as fiercely in return, she would reconsider her position on marriage. Then, oddly choked up by this observation, she slipped off to her room to wash and exchange her dusty riding clothes for a crisp black sateen skirt and a white shirtwaist with a high, lace collar. She didn't have to relax her standards, she concluded, just because she was living in the untamed West now.

By the time he went to bed that night, Toby had not only been bathed, but measured for new clothes, and June-bug was busily laying out pattern pieces, cut from old sheets of newsprint. Rachel, long since finished washing the dishes, sat at the end of the same table, a book before her, watching the other woman work. Sewing was a skill Rachel had never truly mastered, and therefore her clothing was all store-bought, and correspondingly expensive. Living on a schoolteacher's salary, she had a very limited wardrobe, and she was full of admiration as she looked on.

Lantern light, added to the glow from the fireplace, gave a cozy air to the large room and caught in the silver strands glimmering in June-bug's thick brown hair.

"Tell me about Trey Hargreaves's wife," Rachel said, and was as appalled as if someone else had made the audacious request.

Mrs. McCaffrey looked up from her labor of love. She'd taken to Toby right off, that was obvious, and he'd taken to her. Rachel just hoped the alliance wouldn't end in heartbreak for June-bug, somewhere down the road, when and if Mike Houghton returned to claim his son.

"I didn't know her, though I've pried a few things out of Jacob. Trey lost her afore he settled out here— died in his arms, or so the story goes. She was shot when some no-goods robbed a general store in Great

Falls—there to buy sugar, she was, poor thing—and after she died, Trey wasn't good for much of anything for a long time." She paused, remembering, then brightened and went on. "That's a fine girl he's got, though, that little Emma. Smart as they come, and pretty, too. Right pretty." She sighed and began cutting out the small pair of trousers.

"And?" Rachel prompted, sensing something left unsaid. She'd already gone barging into the subject; no use sparing the horses now.

June-bug's expression was rueful in the lamplight, and she was still for a long while, as though looking back over time. Finally, she met Rachel's gaze and spoke. "I reckon Emma's going to have a hard time of it all her life."

"Because of her father and the saloon?"

June-bug smiled sadly and shook her head. "No," she said. "Trey was a rogue and a rounder for a long time. Lot of other things, too, I reckon. But he loves that child, and he'd do just about anything he had to do to protect her and keep her happy."

Rachel waited, knowing there was more. Being a motherless child was very difficult, but this, she sensed, was an even greater challenge, whatever it was.

June-bug's hair, worn down around her shoulders in the evening, fell over one shoulder as she worked, but she raised her head when she finally went on. "Emma's mama was a full-blooded Lakota Sioux. Trey called her Summer Song. Must have been a beautiful woman, if that little girl's looks are anything to go by, but out here—well, everyplace, really—folks don't look too kindly on . . . on—"

"Half-breeds?" Rachel said, to get them both past the ugly word. "Are you saying that people around here don't accept Emma Hargreaves as one of them?"

"There's them who will refuse to send their young-'uns to school if she's there. It ain't right, and it makes Trey mad enough to bite nails, but that's the way of it. And her such a precious little thing, too, with a fine mind and a gentle heart."

Rachel wanted to weep. Poor Emma! Not only did she have to deal with ignorance and prejudice, but she had a saloon-keeper for a father. It was in that moment, Rachel would later reflect, and often, that she had decided to make a special project of educating Emma Hargreaves. She knew of a certain Quaker school in Pennsylvania, where children like Emma were welcomed, and taught to rise, through learning and confidence in themselves and God, above things that might otherwise have held them back. Still, to gain admittance, not to mention a scholarship, Emma would have to score very highly in her studies and prove herself deserving.

"You look so sad," June-bug said, with a tender smile. "It ain't all sorrowful, you know. That little girl is happy, for all of it. Maybe it's them Indian ways of hers that see her through—she's got a knack with animals, for instance, like nothin' you've ever seen. And she listens to the wind and the rain, even the snow, like she can hear it sayin' somethin' to her." June-bug put down her scissors and came to sit on the bench, facing Rachel. "Don't make the mistake of feelin' sorry for Emma. You'll wound her for sure if you do."

Rachel smiled. It was good advice, and she meant to take it. "I think I'll turn in," she said, with a sigh. "It's been a long day."

"You lookin' in on the Kildares tomorrow?"

Rachel nodded. "Maybe the Johnsons, too, if I can manage it."

June-bug was pleasantly skeptical. "Them Kildare boys will probably wear you plumb out. Full of the devil, they are, and their daddy don't say much to 'em about the way they act. Yes, Ma'am, you're going to have your hands full with them."

More good news, Rachel thought, but she was a person of almost boundless energy, and she would be more than a match for two little boys, no matter how wild they turned out to be. Perhaps, she reasoned later, it was her preoccupation with Emma Hargreaves that made her overlook the fact that she was tempting fate, and sorely.

When she arose the next morning, dressed in yesterday's riding clothes, which she'd shaken out and brushed carefully the night before, she found Toby already up and around, clad in his new shirt and trousers. He was coming through the doorway with an armload of kindling when Rachel first spotted him.

"Good morning," she said, with a smile.

He beamed at her. "Mornin'," he replied, and sniffed. It was probably wrong, but Rachel found herself hoping his father would never return. She wondered if the boy had a mother somewhere, but did not consider asking. "Miss June-bug's makin' biscuits and sausage gravy for breakfast!" he announced.

Rachel laughed. "That *is* good news," she said. It was barely dawn, and there were a few lamps burning, as well as a leaping fire on the hearth. The delicious aroma of fresh coffee filled the air, though there was no sign of either June-bug or Jacob.

So intent was she on the pleasures of awakening in the midst of a cozy household that she didn't notice the man lying on the bench, sleeping, and nearly sat on him. She jumped up with a start and a gasp; her heart feeling as though it had stuffed itself into the back of her throat.

Toby laughed. "Don't mind him. He's just an old drifter that had a few too many shots of whiskey down at the Brimstone last night. Jacob let him bed down here, 'stead of the barn, case the old coot should want a smoke and set the hay on fire."

Rachel peered at the man, a grizzled fellow, redolent of liquor and sweat and general fustiness. He looked harmless enough, but startled her again by letting out a sudden, loud snore. "Good heavens," she said, alarmed.

The door opened and Jacob came in, with an armload of firewood. "Not much of heaven about poor old Sibley," he commented, but kindly. "He brung news from the Wainwright place, though. They've got a new baby out there, as of yesterday. A little girl they mean to call Rachel—after you, I reckon."

Rachel was overcome. She had never aspired to

such an honor, never dreamed of one, and her knees went so weak for a moment that she almost sat on Sibley for certain. "I must go and see Evangeline," she decided aloud. "Now, today."

"Nobody around to go with you," Jacob pointed out.

Rachel headed for her room, to fetch the paeonia cutting and her cloak. "Then I'll go by myself," she said, and when she came out again, with her things, nobody raised an argument.

CHAPTER

3

RACHEL SADDLED the same ancient draft horse she'd ridden the day before, there in the misty dimness of the station barn, and led the creature out into the early morning. Jacob soon appeared, standing with arms folded.

"Ain't you even going to ask the way?" he inquired in measured tones.

She was occupied with the logistics of transporting that infernal paeonia cutting, but she'd been watching the stationmaster out of the corner of her eye and bracing herself for a more forceful protest than the one he'd offered earlier, inside the station. "No need," she said lightly. "Evangeline and I have been corresponding regularly ever since she and Abigail came out here. She drew me a map once, and I've looked at it so many times over the last four years, I've got it memorized."

"There's Indians out there, unfriendly ones," Jacob said, presumably describing the territory between

Springwater and the Wainwright ranch. "Bobcats and wolves, too. Miss Evangeline had herself a couple of different run-ins with wolves. She ever write you about *that?*"

A shiver wound itself along the length of Rachel's spine. She had indeed received a thorough accounting of those encounters, and she'd had nightmares about them on and off, ever since. Her reaction to that was to strengthen her inner resolve. "Yes," she admitted. "But if I let such things daunt me at every turn—well, I might just as well have stayed home if I was going to do that."

At the sound of an approaching horse, they both turned, and there was Mr. Hargreaves, mounted on his paint gelding. "Mornin'," he said, to all assembled, with a tug at the brim of his hat. "Young Toby tells me you mean to ride out to the Wainwright place, Miss English. Since I'm headed that way anyhow, to fetch my daughter back home, I thought you might allow me the honor of keeping you company."

Rachel couldn't help being glad of an escort, though she was entirely too stubborn to let on. She gave Jacob a narrow look, well aware that the arrangement was a contrived one; obviously, the older man had sent Toby to the Brimstone Saloon, there to prevail upon Mr. Hargreaves to arise from his bed and accompany the reckless tinhorn schoolmarm on her journey. That was, she reflected, if Mr. Hargreaves had ever gone to bed in the first place. He was in need of barbering, as a dark stubble covered his jaw, and his

clothes looked rumpled. Carousing was apparently
untidy work.

"I could not possibly refuse such a generous offer,"
Rachel said, ungenerously.

Trey smiled, showing perfect white teeth, and
touched his hat brim again. He might as well have
said, straight out, that if she wanted to play games, he
would make a worthy opponent. "Here," he said,
riding forward a little and extending a hand, "let me
hold that seedling, or whatever it is, so you can get
into the saddle. I'm expecting more drovers to come
through tonight, and I want to be back in time to see
they get their whiskey and I get their money."

Rachel glowered at him, but she let him take the
paeonia cutting and hoisted herself onto the borrowed
horse's back. As the fates would have it, it was an
utterly ungraceful effort. When she was settled, with
her skirts arranged and her dignity in place, though
still faltering a bit, she took the paeonia back. She
would be almost as glad to get rid of the thing, she
expected, as she would be to see Evangeline again.

"Heaven forbid," she said, "that *anyone* should be
deprived of their proper share of the devil's brew."

Trey rolled his eyes at that. "This might be a long
day," he said, addressing Jacob.

"No doubt it will," Jacob agreed. "Give the Wainwrights our best, and tell 'em we'll come by for a look
at that new baby soon as we have the chance."

Trey smiled and nodded, but without the insolence
he apparently reserved for Rachel. Then he spurred
the paint into a leisurely trot, and Rachel had to

scramble to keep up. Her own elderly mount would never be able to match his fancy gelding's pace, and she figured he well knew it.

He reined in at the edge of the woods and waited with an indulgent expression that made Rachel want to slap him. She had never done another human being violence in her life, and she didn't intend to start then, but the temptation was a sore one all the same.

They passed the first half of the trip in silence, Trey keeping the paint to a reasonable pace with, she suspected, some difficulty. She could see that the horse wanted to break free and run, and she didn't blame it.

"I won't mind if you want to ride on ahead," she said, somewhat stiffly, when they stopped alongside Willow Creek to rest for a few minutes and let both animals drink. "Poor old Sunflower here can't move very fast."

Trey patted Sunflower's neck as she drank, but he was looking up at Rachel, who stood higher on the grassy bank, wishing she'd taken the time to pack some spare clothes. She had nearly two months before classes were scheduled to begin and, while she still wanted to visit all the families of her potential students, there was no reason she couldn't spend a week or even two with Evangeline, if she wouldn't be intruding. Doubtless, her friend could use the help.

"Maybe you and I ought to strike a truce," Trey said, catching her totally by surprise. "I have a few redeeming qualities, you know."

Rachel arched an eyebrow. Truth be told, she thought it would be unwise to get too friendly with a man like Trey Hargreaves. He nettled her, but it was deeper than that. He was the most, well, *male* man she had ever encountered, and he stirred sensations in her that she'd thought were buried forever. Buried with Langdon.

"Such as?" she asked, but she felt a smile play at the corners of her mouth.

He laughed and swatted one thigh with his hat. "Well," he said, "I can beat most anybody at arm wrestling. I've never lost a horse race or a fist fight in my life, and for all that, I have good table manners."

Rachel had to struggle not to smile outright. She folded her arms. "Most impressive," she said.

He stretched out his hand. "Shake?"

She hesitated, then moved forward and reciprocated. "For Emma's sake," she was careful to say, but at his touch, innocent as it was, a rush of heat surged up her arm and raced through her system to spark at every nerve ending. He went on holding her hand for a moment too long, and for a fraction of that time, she honestly thought he was about to kiss her.

It was both a disappointment and a relief when he did not.

"We'd better get rolling," he said, letting his hand fall to his side.

Rachel nodded and turned away, embarrassed by the color she knew was throbbing in her cheeks.

It was mid-afternoon when they climbed a steep

track onto the high meadow Evangeline had written about so often, and Rachel got her first glimpse of the rambling two-story house. Constructed of logs, it boasted glass windows and a shingle roof. Smoke curled from one of the three chimneys, and before Rachel and Trey could even dismount, the front door sprang open and two young girls erupted through the opening, running wildly, gleefully, toward them.

One—good heavens, she'd grown so much that Rachel barely recognized her—was surely Abigail, ten now, and by all accounts a great help to Evangeline. The other, slightly older and taller, had to be Emma. Her blue-black hair flew behind her as she ran barefoot over the stoney grass, and Trey swung down from his horse just in time to catch her up in an embrace. They whirled, and Emma's lovely hair swung around her luminous face like coarse strands of silk glinting in the sun.

Abigail, an uncommonly pretty child herself, with ebony hair and eyes as blue as cobalt, looked up at Rachel with a pleased expression. "You're Rachel, aren't you? Mama's been waiting for you ever so long."

Rachel got down, clasping the paeonia cutting in one hand, and hugged her best friend's daughter warmly. "Yes," she said, blinking back tears. "I'm Rachel. And you're Abigail. How big you've gotten!"

"We have a new baby," Abigail said. "A girl named Rachel Louisa. Papa says we'd better call her Louisa, because things are confused enough around here as it is."

Rachel smiled and turned, one arm around Abigail's shoulders, to look at Emma, who was huddled against Trey's side, watching her with shy curiosity. Perhaps even—or was she merely imagining it—a certain hopefulness. Rachel put out a hand. "Hello," she said. "I'm Miss English. I'll be your teacher, come the last of August."

Emma ventured out of the loose curve of her father's arm, but only tentatively, offering her own hand in return. "How do you do," she said.

"Very well, thank you," Rachel replied. "And you?"

Emma looked back at Trey, as though in silent consultation. Plainly, she distrusted strangers, and perhaps she had good reason to do so. He nodded, very slightly, in encouragement.

"I like to read books," Emma said staunchly. "Did you bring any new ones with you?"

"I did," Rachel told the child. Abigail was tugging at her hand by then, pulling her toward the house.

"Come in and see Mama," said Evangeline's daughter. "She's just *perishing* for the sight of you. She likes my papa a whole lot, but he's a man and she misses being around women."

Trey and Rachel accidentally glanced at each other then, and something indefinable passed between them. Something that made them both look away.

"Where is your pa?" Trey asked Abigail. "I'd like a word with him."

"He's down at the corral, breaking horses," Abigail

answered, still tugging Rachel along in her wake, but looking back at Trey. "Mama won't let Emma and I go down there and watch, either, even if we promise to stay behind the fence. She says he swears too much, but I don't think it's true because Papa is real gentle with horses. I think she's afraid we'll get stepped on some way, like Kathleen Bellweather's baby sister did—"

The chatter went on until they'd reached the front porch, Trey leading both horses behind him. "You get your things ready, if you've a mind to come home," he said to his daughter. "We'll head for town in an hour or so."

Rachel looked up at the sun, troubled, and dug in her heels against Abigail's pulling. "Will you get back before dark?" she asked doubtfully. She told herself the concern she felt was all for Emma's sake; Trey Hargreaves was a grown man, after all, well able to look after himself.

"An hour or two after, I reckon," Trey answered. There was a grin lurking in his eyes. "You worried about me, Miss English?"

She might have said what came to the tip of her tongue—*Not in the least, Mr. Hargreaves*—if Emma hadn't been watching her so intently. "Yes," she said. "And about Emma, of course. It's no mean distance back to Springwater."

One corner of Trey's mouth tilted upwards. "Well, me and Emma, we don't travel quite so slow as you and that old nag of Jacob's. We can cover twice as much ground in half as much time—can't we, Song-bird?" He ruffled his daughter's hair with obvious affection.

Emma beamed up at him and nodded. "I wish we could get a baby, though," she said. "Like the Wainwrights have. Could we get us a baby from someplace, Pa?"

It was Trey's turn to be unsettled; he flushed, along the underside of his neck, looked away, and cleared his throat once before looking back. "Get your things," he said, but gently. "The paint is rarin' for a good run."

Emma dashed to do his bidding, and Rachel let Abigail pull her over the threshold and into a spacious, open parlor, where a massive stone fireplace dominated one wall. There were several good pieces of furniture in view, and the rugs, Rachel knew, had been imported from San Francisco. Evidently, though Evangeline had not said so outright, Scully Wain-wright had prospered well beyond his wife's modest claims, raising cattle and breeding horses.

Evangeline herself came slowly, but not painfully, down the stairs, just then, her face wreathed in smiles. She glowed with a happiness that went far beyond the bearing of a healthy child and Rachel, for just a fraction of a heartbeat, envied her friend for all that she had.

"Rachel!" Evangeline gasped, half laughing and half sobbing, as she reached the bottom of the stairs and held out both arms in welcome. She was wearing a pretty blue wrapper with white piping and velvet slippers to match.

The two women embraced, both of them weeping for joy, and then Evangeline held Rachel away from her, for a good look. "You can't imagine how I've longed to see you again!" she cried.

Rachel laughed, and cried. "Yes, I can," she protested, with a sniffle, "because I've felt the same way." She remembered the paeonia start, which had nearly been crushed in all the fuss, and now looked somewhat travel-worn and bedraggled. "Here," she said, thrusting it at Evangeline, "is your blasted cutting!"

Evangeline laughed—and cried—as she accepted the stem Rachel had carried so far. "Abigail," she said to her daughter, holding it out. "Put this in water, please. And be very, very careful with it."

Abigail nodded and rushed off to do her mother's bidding.

"Sit down," Rachel exhorted Evangeline. "You mustn't tax your strength."

"Nonsense," Evangeline said, with a wave of one hand. "I think it's a mistake for a new mother to lie about in bed. Better to get up and move around. Heaven knows, there's plenty to do. Oh, Rachel, Rachel—what a joy it is to see you!"

They embraced again, and then went into the kitchen, where an elaborate black cookstove stood, chrome gleaming. Abigail had put the paeonia cutting into a fruit jar full of water and set it in the sunny window over the iron sink.

"Shall I make you some tea, Mama?" she asked.

"That would be wonderful, sweetheart," Evangeline responded. "Thank you. Then go upstairs, if you would, and look in on your brother and little Rachel Louisa. If they're awake, then you can bring the baby to me—very, very carefully—and see if J.J. doesn't need his knickers changed."

Presently, the tea was brewed, and it tasted better to Rachel than any she'd had since the day her friend had left Pennsylvania for the Montana Territory, intending to marry her late husband's cousin, a rancher named John Keating. To Evangeline's surprise and, she'd confessed to Rachel in more than one letter, her relief, Keating had been away when she arrived. She'd been met at the Springwater station by his partner, one Scully Wainwright, who brought her and Abigail to the ranch—they'd lived in a cabin down the hill back then—and over the course of that long, difficult winter, Scully and Evangeline had fallen deeply in love. They'd been prepared to part, however, Evangeline being promised to Big John Keating, but then Big John had come back that spring with a bride in tow, and Scully and Evangeline had been free to marry. The match was a good one, and the two had been happy together.

It was a romantic story and just thinking about it made Rachel sigh.

Emma came in lugging a sleepy, blond imp—J.J., of course—on one hip, while Abigail brought the new baby, carrying her with a gentleness that touched

Rachel's heart. There was a great deal of love in this house; the Wainwrights were fortunate people.

Rachel wondered, just for that one admittedly maudlin moment, if it would have been like this for her and Langdon, had he survived the war and come home to marry her, as they'd planned. Once, she'd hoped to have a houseful of children herself, just as Evangeline did, but now she was resigned to putting all her maternal energies into her teaching. It was better that way, she told herself. Look at poor Sue Bellweather; being a mother was dangerous business, emotionally. Maybe as perilous, in this wild and perilous place, as entrusting a lover to the whims of war.

And if she was protesting too much, well, she didn't know quite what to make of that possibility.

"Rachel?" Evangeline said, and Rachel realized that her friend had been trying to get her attention. "Would you like to hold your namesake?"

Some powerful, primitive emotion swept through Rachel as she took the infant from Abigail's arms and held her against her bosom; she was almost overcome by it. The baby girl was incomprehensibly beautiful, with an aura of fine golden hair and ivory-pink skin, and she blinked up at Rachel with an endearing expression of bafflement, her tiny fingers grasping at air. "Her eyes are blue," Rachel said, somewhat stupidly.

"All newborns have blue eyes," Evangeline reminded her, but gently.

Rachel had to swallow hard not to weep, partly in

celebration of this new and wonderful little life, and partly in mourning for the children she herself would never bear, never hold against her heart, never nurture at her breast. Suddenly, she wanted desperately to have a home of her own, a flock of lively children. Which meant, of course, she'd need a husband.

"I've got my things ready, Pa," Emma said, startling Rachel into looking up from the baby's face. She saw Trey standing just inside the kitchen doorway, hat in hand, staring at Rachel as though he'd never seen a woman holding an infant before. "Just let me get J.J. a piece of sugar bread, and we can go."

Evangeline looked from Trey to Rachel, and back to Trey. Her expression was a puzzled one, at first, but then a slow smile blossomed on her mouth. "You ought to stay for supper, Trey. Or even spend the night. It's a long way back to Springwater."

Trey hesitated, then shook his head. "I don't guess we'd better do that," he said. "But thank you for the invitation. Thanks too for takin' such good care of Emma."

Evangeline smiled fondly at the child. "She's a treasure. We'll miss you very much, Emma. You've been a great help."

Emma looked pleased. "I like babies," she said. "I want to get one."

Evangeline stopped smiling, but Rachel could see that it was an effort. Her friend's gray eyes were bright with tender amusement. "What you need," she told the child, though she was watching Trey the whole time she spoke, "is a stepmother." She let that sink in

for a few moments, then addressed Trey directly.
"Those rooms above the saloon could surely use a
woman's touch."

Rachel thought a round of cannon-fire would
probably be more in order, given the way most men
kept house, but she wouldn't have said so, not in front
of Emma and Abigail, at least. She turned her
attention back to the baby and immediately found
herself enthralled all over again.

Trey and Emma said their good-byes and left, and
Evangeline stood up to start supper. Rachel sat her
back down again, gave her the baby to nurse, and
went about preparing the meal herself.

Scully came in from outside when the food was
ready. He was just as Evangeline had described him,
handsome, in a rugged and somewhat alarmingly
masculine way, with turquoise eyes and sun-bronzed
skin. The way he looked at Evangeline revealed the
depths of his love for her, and that endeared him to
Rachel as nothing else could have done.

"Rachel," Evangeline said proudly, the baby sleeping on her shoulder, "this is my husband, Scully
Wainwright. Scully, here is my Rachel, at long, long
last."

He smiled, moved to offer his hand, and then drew
it back again. "I reckon I ought to wash up first," he
said. "We're pleased to have you, Miss English. I hope
you can stay awhile, as Evangeline has surely missed
your company."

Rachel flushed. Scully was a charming man and he,
like Trey Hargreaves, made poor lost Langdon

seem, well . . . bland, by comparison. "I'll stay a few days, if I won't be in the way," she said, feeling uncommonly shy.

"I won't let you go before a week is out, at least," Evangeline told her, as Scully left the room, presumably to wash. "I'm sure it will take you the better part of the week to tell me all about the last four years, and besides that, I did up the spare room with you in mind. The least you can do is put it to use."

Rachel laughed. "You've always been one to make a strong case," she said.

Scully returned, shining with cleanliness. "Eve would make a fine lawyer," he said, and bent to kiss his wife's glowing cheek. "If we could spare her, that is. Which we can't." Why did the sight of him, the sound of him, make Rachel wish that Trey Hargreaves had stayed, at least for supper? It made no sense at all, given that she didn't *like* Mr. Hargreaves even a little.

Well, maybe a little.

Supper proved to be a lively event in the Wainwright household, with the baby gurgling and Abigail chattering and young J.J. waving a spoonful of mashed and buttery turnips in a precarious arc around his head. Evangeline oversaw the whole meal with ease and once again Rachel found herself envying her friend, as well as admiring her.

What would it be like, she wondered, to live so richly, so fully, so well? Inwardly, she sighed. She might never know, and she'd better accept the fact with as much good grace as she could muster, make the best of things, and get on with her life. As a teacher, after all, she was in a position to make a genuine difference to a great many children, and she wanted to pursue that end as much as she ever had. The problem was that she wanted so much *more*, wanted things she hadn't allowed herself to dream about since the news of Langdon's cruel death had reached her.

That night, alone in the lovingly prepared spare room of which Evangeline was justifiably proud, the house dark and quiet around her, Rachel wept.

Perhaps she truly *might* have a second opportunity to find happiness—Evangeline, after all, had once counted her own life as over, at least in terms of loving and being loved by a man. Then she'd met Scully.

On the other hand, Rachel reminded herself, with a soft sniffle, hers was a slightly different position than Evangeline's. Her friend had been a widow, an honorable state of being. Unmarried women, however, were expected to be virgins, and Rachel wasn't. She'd lain with Langdon, and she could not rightly say she was sorry, for she had cared for him deeply. Still, a great many men, even ones with reputations of their own, like Trey, would not even consider taking a bride who'd known another man first.

Just the thought of being shamed and rejected like that made Rachel's cheeks burn with humiliation.

She must get a hold of herself, stop fussing and fretting and carrying on like some actress in a bad play. It was only that she was overwrought, finally seeing her friend after anticipating the event for so long, holding the baby that was her namesake in her arms.

Nothing to do with Trey.

But it was more, and she knew that, and furthermore, she knew it had *everything* to do with Mr. Hargreaves, which was the most disturbing realization of all.

He developed a habit, over the eight long and enlightening days of her absence, of standing at one of the upstairs windows, usually the one nearest his desk, and staring down at the empty schoolhouse and waiting. Watching, like some kind of addlepated fool. And when he wasn't watching and waiting, he was thinking about her. Not about the wife who'd died so tragically, not about the lost years he'd spent mourning her, hating her killers, searching for them. Finding them.

Not about what he'd done, to avenge his wife.

The impossible had happened: Trey had found space in his heart for Rachel English—in fact, he loved her as he had never loved any other woman, including Emma's mother. Wanted her for his own. She was, he reckoned, the first female he'd *ever* wanted that he couldn't have, just by asking.

Not that mapping out the true landscape of his soul for the first time made any real difference; Rachel had made her opinions clear, where he was concerned. She wouldn't have a saloon-keeper for a husband, let alone one with a past like his. He wished, in those moments, that he could go back and change almost everything he'd ever done, make himself into a different, better man, one worthy of a prize like Rachel.

It made his gut grind, just to imagine her going away, or marrying someone else. She was meant to be his—he knew it. The question was, did *she* know?

To distract himself from thoughts of Rachel, from the memory of the revenge he'd taken on Summer Song's murderers, he turned his mind toward his daughter. Emma, who had reshaped his life around just by needing him, who had clutched at his sleeve when he presented himself in Choteau for Miss Ionie's funeral and begged him to take her home with him. That was when he'd settled down; he'd had to make a home, before he had one to offer Emma, but he'd done it. Such as it was, he reflected, glancing around ruefully.

She'd heard about Miss English's visit to the Bell-weather house, Emma had, and she was hankering for a social call of her own, complete with tea and cookies. At first, Trey had been at his wits' end, thinking about that—he didn't have the first idea how to make tea, and he'd sooner have wrestled a grizzly than try to bake up a batch of cookies. Emma, for all her brains and her book learning, spent every free hour outside, running the countryside like a wolf cub, and she was probably a worse cook than he was, if that was possible. Generally, the bartender, Zeke, made their vittles, but he wasn't up to anything fancier than cornbread and fried meat.

It caused Trey no little bit of anguish to know his daughter wanted something so much, something he might not be able to give her. It probably signified approval to her, a fancy visit from the schoolmarm, and she asked for so little, Emma did. The thought of disappointing her made him ache.

It was a while before it came to him to approach Miss June-bug with the idea of doing up the fixings, when the time came, so that Emma would not be shamed. Not, he thought, that Miss Rachel English was one to embarrass a child—no, sir, she reserved her humiliations for grown men.

Miss June-bug agreed to the cookie-baking and tea-brewing, for she was a kindly and charitable woman, for all that she would have burned his saloon right down to the ground if she could have gotten leave from the Lord, and that was a weight off Trey's mind. It was odd, then, that he went right on fretting about the matter and watching at the window for Rachel to return. He'd go and speak to her about Emma as soon as he got the chance.

On the afternoon of the eighth day, she turned up, escorted by Scully Wainwright. She was traveling aboard the pitiful old nag Jacob had given her the use of, while Scully rode that fine Appaloosa gelding of his. They dismounted in front of the schoolhouse, tied their horses to the teetering hitching rail, and went inside.

Trey watched for them to come out, and when they did, Miss Rachel standing on the step smiling and waving, Scully swinging back up onto the Appaloosa's back to ride away, he practically killed himself bounding down the stairs and through the saloon proper to burst out through the swinging doors like a man with a mighty purpose.

Rachel, still standing on the schoolhouse step, looked a little startled, as though she might be considering dodging inside and latching the door after her. Trey slowed his steps, for the sake of his own self-respect as much as her reassurance, or so he told himself.

"You're back," he said, and silently cursed himself for a raving fool. Of *course* she was back. She was standing right there in plain sight, wasn't she?

She smiled, and there was something soft in her face that nettled even more than the usual mockery. Trey resisted an urge to take a step back, like some kind of yellow-belly. "I had a wonderful visit," she said, "but I've got things to do here. Evangeline is up and about and so full of energy, you'd never know she just had a baby." Color flooded her face the instant the words were out of her mouth; no doubt, for an Eastern schoolmarm, it wasn't proper to mention such things in mixed company.

Trey decided to let the misstep pass, since he was so nervous himself and besides that, he wanted something. He stood just outside the fence, a little to the left of her swaybacked horse, both thumbs hooked in his belt so she might not see his hands shaking.

"My daughter Emma heard about your visiting the Bellweathers," he said bluntly. Might as well just spit it out and get it over with. "She's got her heart set on your coming to call on—on her." He'd almost said "on us," instead, but he caught himself just in time. He saw her eyes rise to take in the saloon, looming like Judgment Day itself behind him. He swallowed, thinking he'd be at a loss for what to do if she refused. Emma would be crushed.

"I'd be happy to visit Emma," she said.

He stared at her. Having been braced for a rebuff, he was unprepared for an acceptance. "Oh, well, when?" he stumbled out, once his own face had had time to turn good and red.

"Whenever it's convenient," she answered blithely. "Tomorrow afternoon, perhaps?"

Trey swallowed, thinking of the rough accommodations he and his daughter shared. There was only one bedroom, and that was Emma's. He was usually downstairs half the night, and when he did sleep, he just stretched out on the old couch next to the stove. They had no fancy dishes, and no pictures on the walls, unless you counted the page Emma had torn from a wall calendar, a few years before, a simple rendering of an Indian girl on a pony, watching the moon rise. "Tomorrow afternoon," he echoed, and damn near choked on the words.

"Two o'clock?" she prompted. He couldn't tell if she was laughing at him or not, behind that placid schoolmarm expression on her face, and at the moment he didn't care. She was coming for a visit, and Emma would not be let down. For the time being, nothing else mattered. Nothing in the world.

"Two o'clock," he said, and turned to go so fast that he damn near stumbled over his own feet and landed face down in a puddle of rainwater, mud, and horsepiss. As it was, Jacob McCaffrey almost ran him down with a buckboard.

CHAPTER

4

RACHEL HAD DONNED her best clothes—the black sateen skirt and snowy white shirtwaist—for the call on the Hargreaves household. Her hair was done up in a tidy chignon and she walked proudly, briskly, as was her normal way, with her chin up and her gaze fixed straight ahead.

In front of the Brimstone Saloon, she stopped and debated her means of entrance. Odd that she hadn't thought of this before, she reflected uneasily. Visiting a student was one thing, but walking straight through the front doors of such a place in the broad light of day was entirely another. Schoolteachers were held to exceedingly high standards of morality and personal decorum, and many had been dismissed for far lesser infractions. Perhaps, she thought, chewing her lower lip, there was a rear door.

"Changing your mind?" Trey asked, nearly startling her out of her skin. He stood just inside, and held one of the swinging doors aside for her. "This is mighty important to Emma."

Rachel was indignant at the mere suggestion that she would have been so rude as to turn around and flee at the very threshold of a pupil's home. "I was merely wondering," she said, keeping her voice low in case the child was nearby, "if there was another way in."

A grin spread across Trey's face. "Well," he said, "as it happens, there is. You might have found it, if you'd bothered to look behind the saloon. It's been my experience that rear doors are almost always situated in the back of a building. However, since you've already made a spectacle of yourself, you might as well come right on in."

Rachel passed him with a regal stride, which was not easy, given her rather *un*regal size of five feet, two inches. She glanced about curiously, once inside, for of course she had never set foot in an establishment of that sort before, and she collected and treasured new impressions the way other people gathered postage stamps or pressed flowers for their scrapbooks.

No lamps were lit, and the shadowy dimness lent the long room an air of mystery, not unlike the innermost parts of a harem, or the secret chamber in some fairy-tale castle. There were two large tables, for billiards or pool, along with a number of smaller ones, some with bare tops, others covered in felt. A roulette wheel took up a good part of one wall, giving the lie to Rachel's own naive assumption that there was no gambling going on beneath Trey's roof, and the bar itself seemed as long as a boxcar, with a glistening mirror behind it. Although she naturally had no standard by which to judge it all, Rachel was sure that the Brimstone was especially well-appointed, for a Western drinking hall. A few customers, careful to keep their heads ducked and their hat brims pulled low, lingered here and there, in isolated silence, nursing their drinks.

Out of the corner of her eye, Rachel could see that Trey was enjoying her discomfiture, try though she had to hide it from him, and that stirred an irritation in her that she wouldn't even have *tried* to master, if she hadn't known how very important this visit was to Emma. June-bug had been baking all morning, and just over an hour ago she'd sent Toby to the Brimstone with her only tea set, as well as enough molasses-oatmeal cookies to feed the nearest cavalry regiment. Toby's reward, upon returning from this errand, had been a feast of sweets that had left him rolling on his cot and holding his belly. Jacob was planning to lecture him on the virtues of moderation, and the McCaffreys themselves had had words over the incident, Jacob maintaining that encouraging greed was no favor to the child, June-bug retorting that the poor little scamp probably hadn't had anybody to fuss over him in the whole of his life.

Just as Rachel's eyes were adjusting to the light, she caught a glimpse of Emma, standing at the top of the stairway at the back of the room. The little girl had tied a blue ribbon in her hair, to match the pretty calico dress she'd worn for the occasion, and her smile was so tentative, so eager, that Rachel immediately put aside all her differences with Trey and focused her attention on the child.

"Emma," she said, "you look *very* lovely."

Emma's long, raven-dark eyelashes lowered, just for a moment, in shy pleasure. "Thank you, Miss English," she said. "We've got cookies. And tea, too. At least, we will have, once I pour hot water over the leaves of orange pekoe in Mrs. McCaffrey's china pot."

Rachel went willingly up the stairs, Trey close behind her. "I have been anticipating this visit ever since your father invited me yesterday," she said. "Tell me, Emma, what is your favorite subject in school? I know you like to read—you told me that when I first met you, at the Wainwright ranch. But what else do you enjoy? History? Geography? Ciphering?"

Emma's dark eyes were alight. "I like writing, Miss English. I want to make books someday."

Rachel reached the landing, and barely stayed herself from embracing the child. It was important to tread carefully, when meeting with new students, especially sensitive ones, like Emma. She might misinterpret an overly avid interest as condescension or pity, and if that happened, the delicate rapport between teacher and pupil could be damaged beyond repair. "What sort of books?" She laid a hand on Emma's shoulder and allowed the little girl to lead her into the living area she and her father shared. "True ones, or stories?"

Emma fairly glowed. "Stories," she confided, with a note of wonder.

"Then we must center our efforts on your composition skills," Rachel said. "Though, mind you, arithmetic and history are important, too, as is geography. We can't give those subjects short shrift."

"Short how-much?" Emma asked, brow furrowed.

Rachel explained the meaning of the phrase, and found herself in the midst of a pleasant if simply furnished room. Three chairs had been drawn up to a worn but solid-looking oaken table, and June-bug's cheerful tea service was set out with such care that Rachel's heart tightened for a moment, just to look at it. A plate of the savory cookies was on prominent display as well. There was no cookstove—merely a potbellied affair with a black kettle on top—and no settee or decorations of any kind, save a tattered calendar page showing a young Indian girl on a spotted pony silhouetted against a giant moon.

It wasn't difficult to work out why Emma would favor such an image, of course; she was proud of her heritage, and Rachel was glad to know it. Too many children of mixed ancestry, and adults as well, were treated as if they were inferior to others. The decision of whether or not to accept that assessment of one's self, however, in Rachel's considered opinion at least, remained a matter of personal choice.

Trey cleared his throat, and Rachel turned to look at him. He was obviously uncomfortable with the whole fuss—her presence, the china tea things borrowed from June-bug, perhaps even the cookies—but he was willing to endure it all for Emma's sake. Knowing that made Rachel think better of the man—

though only slightly, she decided. If he was really as interested in giving his daughter a normal life as he made himself out to be, would he be willing to raise her over a saloon?

And were those bullet holes, there in the wall next to the stove? Rachel squinted, uncertain.

Emma dragged back one of the chairs, the place of honor, Rachel suspected. Her small face was bright and earnest. "Sit down, Teacher." She glanced up at her father, whose face Rachel could not see, since he was standing just behind her. "I mean, *please* sit down."

Rachel made something of a show of settling herself in the chair; it was an occasion for Emma, and for that reason she would savor every moment, every sip of tea. She would certainly consume at least one of the cookies as well, even though they were the size of saucers and sure to spoil her supper. "Thank you," she said.

"Now you can sit down, Pa," Emma told Trey. Some of the child's anxiety had ebbed away, but her eyes were still bright with pleasure.

"Thanks—er, thank you very much," Trey replied, with an elegant bow to his daughter, who beamed in delight. What an engaging child Emma was, Rachel thought, with yet another twinge in her heart.

When Trey was seated, Emma got the tea kettle from the stove, using both hands and a dish towel to grasp the handle, and lugged the steaming water over to the table, there to fill June-bug's china pot. Rachel sensed that Trey was poised to leap, in case the child's hold should slip, as she was herself, but in the end it was a good thing neither of them moved. Emma managed the task on her own, with an awkward competence.

Although Rachel would often, over a period of many years, try to recall the conversation that followed, somehow it always remained elusive and somehow magical, like the shadow of a unicorn, barely glimpsed at the edge of a moon-splashed clearing. She remembered that they laughed, the three of them, and surely they must have talked about school and lessons, but Rachel could never call the precise words and topics back to her mind.

At the end of the visit, she and Emma were fast and lifelong friends, although she still had her reservations about Trey. He was an enigma, a purveyor of whiskey and the lord of a gambling den, and yet he was plainly an attentive parent. Few men of his inclinations, Rachel knew, would have endured a tea party on any account.

Good-byes were said, and Rachel rose to leave, this time by the rear door, belated as that effort seemed. Emma, humming under her breath, carefully cleared away the remains of the cookies and tea, while Trey escorted their guest down the back stairs.

"Mr. Hargreaves," Rachel said, when they reached what would have been an alley, had there been any other buildings around, "you have raised a remarkable daughter."

"Thank you."

"I don't mind telling you that it still worries me,

though, her growing up in a saloon." She was thinking of the bullet holes again, the ones in the wall by the stove. If indeed that was what they were.

Trey's eyes narrowed a little, and some of the luster went off his grin. "We live real simple, Miss English," he said, "but Emma's getting a decent raising. You don't believe me, you just ask Miss June-bug. She's no great admirer of mine, Jacob's missus, but even she will tell you that I look after my little girl. For one thing, maybe you didn't notice, but Emma's got shoes on her feet, good ones, and when your pupils start trailing in toward the last of August, you'll find out that's uncommon out here. Most of those kids will be lucky to have shoes before it snows."

Rachel rested her hands on her hips. "I'm not implying that you don't provide for Emma," she said, in a conscientious whisper, "nor do I doubt for a moment that you love her. What concerns me is," she gestured toward the hulking saloon, "this . . . this *place*. Mr. Hargreaves, I am admittedly a greenhorn, but I do know bullet holes when I see them. Surely you can imagine the danger to Emma—"

Trey's jaw clamped down hard, and she watched, fascinated and a little unnerved, as he made a visible effort to relax it. "Emma did that herself, playing with one of my pistols six months back. It was the first and last time I ever paddled her. Good God, do you think I'm just going to stand there and let some drifter empty a pistol into the place where my daughter lives?"

Rachel drew a deep breath and let it out slowly.

He'd convinced her by the sheer righteous indignation of his response. "Perhaps I have been a bit unreasonable—"

"A *bit* unreasonable? You practically came right out and said you don't trust me to take care of my own child!"

Rachel closed her eyes for a moment. "I'm sorry. I didn't mean—" she paused miserably. "It's just that—"

Trey released a sharp sigh and looked exasperated, though whether with her or with himself, she couldn't quite tell. Maybe it was a little of both. "I guess I might have reacted a mite too strongly myself," he surprised her by admitting. "It's just that usually, when folks feel called upon to express an opinion about Emma's raising, they say I ought to send her away again, to some school, maybe. I don't cotton to that kind of interference."

Rachel, calm again, back in control of herself, held up a hand to snag a certain phrase from the stream of what he'd just said. "Just a moment. What do you mean, 'send her away *again*'? Are you saying that you didn't raise Emma?"

He looked away, then back again. "Up until she was eight, Emma lived with my mother's people, over in Choteau—specifically her second cousin Jimpson's widow, Miss Ionie. Miss Ionie was old, though, and she passed on four years ago, so I brought Emma home. She's been with me since then."

Rachel stood there, absorbing all that she'd just heard. Perhaps she'd been too hasty in giving Trey credit for his daughter's intelligence and good manners, she concluded. Perhaps it was the late Mrs. Jimpson who had deserved the acclaim. "I see," she said.

"No," Trey argued quietly, sharply, "you *don't* see. You probably figure I wanted to be shut of Emma so I could have myself a high old time building my saloon. The fact is, she was only a baby when her mother died, and I was out of my mind with grief. I asked Miss Ionie to take Emma in and she did, God rest her soul. But there was never a day of the time we were apart, Emma and I, that I didn't think of her and wish I could bring her here to be with me."

"But you didn't," Rachel said, without rancor. "Not until Miss Ionie died and you had no other choice."

"It wasn't like that, damn it!" Trey snapped.

"I believe you!" Rachel snapped back, and was surprised to realize it was true. Which wasn't to say she didn't still have concerns for Emma's safety and well-being. It might be prudent, she decided, to alter the course of present conversation. "Perhaps you could build a house, just a small one—"

Trey made a move to snatch his hat off and slap it against his thigh, something Rachel had already cataloged as one of the gestures he made when he was exasperated, but the whole exercise was futile because he wasn't wearing a hat. "I'm not Scully Wainwright," he said. "I've got practically every cent I have tied up in that saloon!"

Rachel frowned. "What on earth does Scully have to do with this?"

"He's got a fine, fancy house. Horses and cattle. Money."

"And?"

"And I don't have any of those things. Not yet, anyway, though I mean to get them, you can be sure of that. Until I do, Teacher, Emma and I are going to go right on living in those rooms up there." He cocked a thumb over his shoulder without looking back. "If you've got any other opinions to offer, I'd appreciate it if you'd just keep them to yourself!"

"You really are irascible," Rachel said, her hands back on her hips. "I'm sorry we started this conversation at all." It had, after all, gotten them nowhere.

"So am I," Trey bit out. Then he turned on one boot heel and stormed away, and so ended the first and almost certainly the last tea party ever held within the walls of the Brimstone Saloon.

"Well?" June-bug demanded eagerly, the moment Rachel set foot inside the station. "How did things go, over there at Trey's place?"

Rachel frowned, wondering what her friend expected of a simple student-teacher visit. She'd seen something of the same attitude in Evangeline, on that first evening at the ranch, a watchfulness where she and Trey were concerned. A subtle but still unsettling interest in the lively dynamics between them.

Rachel shrugged, although she did not cherish a

single hope that the gesture would circumvent June-bug's curiosity. "It all went very well," she said, approaching a table set square in a spill of daylight from a high window, where the other woman was busy cutting out another pair of boy-sized trousers. "You were right about Emma. She really is a special child— the sort a teacher comes across only once or twice in a career, I suspect."

June-bug nodded. She wasn't dismissing Emma's exceptional qualities by refraining from comment, Rachel knew; the other woman had accepted them as fact, long since, and probably saw no need to elaborate. "And Trey? Did he stick it out, or head for the hills?"

At last, Rachel smiled. "He *wanted* to run like a rabbit," she confided, "but he stayed for Emma. It was a little like watching a man try to sit still in the middle of a bonfire."

June-bug laughed. "He's a hand with the women, Trey is, but I reckon its been a spell since he sat himself down to take tea and cookies with a pair of respectable females. My goodness, I'd have given a good laying-hen to see that."

Rachel glanced toward the closed door of the small room behind the cook stove, where Toby slept. "How is the boy?"

June-bug gave a fond smile. "He'll be all right. Just et too many cookies, poor little feller. Now that he's done chuckin' 'em up, he ought to get better right fast."

Shaking her head, Rachel proceeded to her room, where she changed out of her good clothes and into a plain calico dress, suited to working around the station. When she was at her sewing, which was often now, June-bug was willing to accept a helping hand.

The following morning, directly after breakfast, Rachel packed herself a sandwich and a bottle of tea, saddled Sunflower, and set out on her visiting rounds, choosing the Kildare place for her first stop. Mr. Kildare was a widower, she recalled, consulting the notes she carried in the pocket of her riding skirt, with two young sons. Someone, precisely who she could not then recall, had warned her about the Kildare boys, but she was not concerned. In a decade of teaching, Rachel had encountered a great variety of children, and she'd never been bested by a single one of them.

She was thinking not of her future pupils, but of Trey Hargreaves, when the Kildare ranch house came into view. It was a small place, but more prosperous looking than the Bellweathers', with a painted barn and two horses, one black with three white boots and a blaze on its nose, the other a smaller sorrel, prancing in the corral.

Her heart nearly stopped beating when two lithe little shapes dropped from the branches of the leafy birches she was passing between, shrieking like wild Indians on the warpath. The boys were the spitting image of each other, covered with freckles, their hair carrot red and shaggy. They wore nothing except loincloths improvised from flour sacks, and they had painted themselves with streaks of what Rachel devoutly hoped was berry juice. War paint, no doubt.

"Halt!" commanded the smaller of the pair. The difference in height was so marginal as to be barely discernible. "Who goes there?"

Rachel took a few moments to school her mouth, which wanted to laugh, now that her heart had settled back into its normal place. She introduced herself, as seriously as possible, adding, "I'm the new schoolteacher."

The larger savage spat with truly splendid contempt. "Pshaw!" he cried.

Who goes there? Pshaw? What sort of Indians were these? Again, Rachel had to work to contain her amusement. There was nothing to be accomplished, ever, by making a child feel foolish. "Nonetheless," she said, with all the dignity of a noble captive facing certain death at the hands of barbarians. For all she knew, they meant to lash her to a tree and build a bonfire at her feet. "You will be attending class as of the last week in August. I'm afraid you'll have to wear trousers and shirts, though. Loincloths are not acceptable."

The savages looked at each other in plain consternation.

"I would like to speak with your father," Rachel went on, when the silence lengthened. "Is he here, please?"

The smaller Indian gave a despondent wave toward

the barn. "He's out back, shoeing a horse," he said, sagging at the shoulders.

Rachel got down from Sunflower's back and held out a hand. "How do you do," she said, addressing the nearest boy. "Would you be Jamie, or Marcus Aurelius?"

One of the lads burst into such raucous laughter that he doubled over with it, while the other blushed furiously behind his freckles. The laughing boy was Jamie, then, Rachel concluded, and the embarrassed one was Marcus Aurelius.

She was proved right in the next instant. The red-faced Indian stepped forward to accept her hand, however tentatively, and give it a brief shake. "Just Marcus," he said.

"All right, then," Rachel said, still keeping a straight face, "so it shall be. Marcus, I am pleased to meet you." She turned to Jamie. "And you, as well," she added.

Jamie remained where he was, hands clasped behind his back, eyes narrow and suspicious. "I don't need to go to school," he said. "I can already read and write and count to a thousand. Ma taught me." He glanced at Marcus. "Taught us both."

"Ma's gone," Marcus pointed out to his brother, none too gently, "and there's a heap we still don't know. I stand in favor of it. Going to school, I mean."

"A wise choice," Rachel said sagely. Looking up, she saw a man coming toward her, a broad smile on his face. He was dressed in work clothes, of course, and perhaps thirty years of age, with twinkling hazel-colored eyes and a headful of thick brown hair, lightly streaked by the sun, as if he often worked without a hat.

"How-do," he said. "I'm Landry Kildare. These galoots, I guess you know by now, are my boys, Jamie and Marcus—"

"Just Marcus," the latter put in quickly, pointedly.

Mr. Kildare's very fetching smile widened. "Just Marcus, then," he agreed.

"Rachel English," Rachel replied. "I hope I'm not intruding. I've just come by to introduce myself and to tell you that classes will begin on the last Monday in August."

"It would be an honor if you'd step inside and have some coffee, Miss English," Kildare said, in his cheerful and mannerly way. Rachel wondered where he came from originally, for she could not recognize any particular accent to his speech. "We don't get too many visitors out our way. Hope these little scoundrels didn't scare you out of your hide. They've got a bad habit of dressing up like African cannibals and jumping out of trees when somebody comes toward the house. Like to have sent poor old Calvin T. Murdoch, the peddler, splashing over the Jordan River into the arms of his Savior."

Leading Sunflower by the reins, Rachel found herself walking alongside Landry Kildare. It was a wonder, in this wild and desolate place, that such an attractive and personable man should go unmarried. June-bug had told her little about him though, merely saying that he was friendly enough when a person met up with him but kept to himself most of the time, so for all Rachel knew, he already had a lady-friend somewhere.

The inside of the cabin was surprisingly tidy and well-furnished, given that this was a household of men. The wooden floors were not only planed smooth, but polished, and there was a colorful, if very worn, scatter rug in front of the hearth. Closed doors indicated several bedrooms, and the area surrounding the cookstove was as clean as if it had been scrubbed down with soapy water and a hard-bristled brush.

"Have a seat, if you'd like," Landry said, indicating a sturdy rocking chair facing the fireplace. Beside the chair, on an upturned fruit crate, was an open book— *Curwen's the Husbandry of Horses*—a cherrywood pipe, and a small tin of tobacco. "Might be you'd rather stand, after riding out from Springwater."

Rachel did prefer to stand; her legs *were* a little cramped.

"I could make some coffee," Landry offered once again, washing his hands at a basin near the stove.

Rachel was about to refuse when she realized that it was important to him to offer hospitality. Visitors, as he'd said, were rare. "I'd like that," she said.

He dismissed the boys, who were plainly eager to get back to their marauding, and made himself busy, putting a small amount of water in the bottom of the large enameled pot, measuring in some coffee grounds, and setting the concoction on the stove. When he was finished building up the fire, he crossed the room and drew up the only other chair to sit astraddle of it, his arms resting easily across the back, looking up at Rachel with those strangely guileless eyes.

If she had to be drawn to a man, if she had to endure all the sweet, secret stirrings, the conflicts and heartaches, why couldn't it have been someone like Landry Kildare, instead of Trey? There was certainly nothing romantic about her instant affection for Kildare, however—it was strictly that of a friend for a friend or, at most, a sister for a brother.

"I reckon you've already discerned that you're going to have your hands full with my boys," Landry said, with a twitch at the corner of his mouth and a light in his eyes. In a flash of insight, Rachel knew that he'd been exactly the same sort of rascal when he was young as his children were now.

Rachel permitted herself the particular smile of amusement she could not have indulged in front of Jamie and Marcus. "I'm up to the challenge," she said, but modestly.

Landry's eyes clouded briefly with memories. "They run wild around this place, I've got to admit that. Since their mother passed over, well, I haven't had the heart to rein them in much. The devil of it is, Caroline would strip my hide off if she saw how they are now, with no manners and all."

"They're good boys," Rachel said quietly.

Landry nodded. "That they are. But what kind of men will they grow up to be, with no proper church-

ing, and them just starting to go to school at eight and
ten years old? Caroline always schooled them, and she
taught them well, but I don't know that there's
another human being in all God's creation who could
get those two to sit still and listen for the better part of
a day, let alone 'most *every* day, and for months at a
stretch."

"We'll manage," Rachel assured him. She felt
slightly less confident, however, than she made herself
out to be.

The coffee began to boil, richly fragrant, and
Landry got up to add cold water and a dash of salt, to
settle the grounds. When that was done, he poured
them each a cup, adding generous portions of fresh
cream and brown sugar, with Rachel's permission,
before serving the brew. It was delicious, and Rachel
was glad she'd accepted Landry's offer of refreshment,
for the concoction braced her up a little. When she
left the Kildares, she would visit the Johnsons, the last
and most remote family, living in a hollow higher up,
in the hill country. The household, like that of the
Bellweathers, had just one child, a girl called Christabel according to June-bug, a shy and skittish little
thing, with one club foot.

After saying her farewells to Jamie and Marcus, as
well as to their father, of course, Rachel mounted
Sunflower again and set out. She ate the sandwich
she'd packed at the station as she rode up and up,
deeper and deeper into the wilderness, home of wolves
and grizzly bears and mountain lions.

The silence was underlaid with a hundred different sounds—birds, small animals rustling in the brush, twigs snapping. She strained to hear each one, to separate it out from the others and identify it. By the time the Johnson shack came into view, Rachel was full of foreboding.

CHAPTER

5

A SHOTGUN BLAST rent the air, loud enough to split the sky. Sunflower tossed her head and pranced in agitation, while Rachel struggled to rein her in. In the process, the bottle in which she'd carried her tea fell to the hardscrabble ground and splintered. A crone-like woman stood on the slanted stoop of the Johnsons' tumbledown shed of a house, shotgun in hand. Smoke curled blue from the barrel.

"That's jest about fer enough!" yelled the old woman.

Rachel's initial fear had given way to supreme irritation by the time she'd calmed the horse. Fretful that the animal would step on the shards of glass and cut one of the soft pads inside her hooves, she got down and tried to kick and scuff the remains of June-bug's bottle aside as best she could. That done, she faced the welcoming committee with hands on hips. "Put that thing away," she commanded, in her most authoritative schoolmarmly tone, "before someone gets hurt."

Evidently Mrs. Johnson, or whoever she was, had never been to school, for she did not seem intimidated. In fact, she balanced the considerable weight of that shotgun as easily and as expertly as any man Rachel had ever seen. "Nobody bound to get hurt but you, Miss. Now you take that sorry excuse fer a hoss and git."

Rachel tethered Sunflower to a sturdy bush, well away from the place where the bottle had landed, and took a few purposeful steps forward. "You just go ahead and shoot me, then. I'm not leaving until I've done what I came here to do!"

For an interval that might have been the length of either a heartbeat or a season, the two adversaries just stared at each other, each one waiting in vain for her opponent to back down.

"What do you want, then?" the old woman finally demanded. Her hair was snow white, her eyes brown, and all but lost in the loose and weathered flesh of her face. She was small of stature, and probably didn't weigh much more than a wet barn cat. "Spit it out and git."

Rachel cleared her throat and squared her shoulders. She'd made a lot of home visits in her time, but she'd never been met with a shotgun before. She wanted to choose her words carefully. "My name is Rachel English, and I'm the new schoolteacher. I'd like to see Christabel and her mother or father."

The old lady spat. "Her pa got hisself hanged over

in Virginia City five years back. God only knows where her ma might be by now. Probably took up with another waster by this time, if she's still breathin'."

Rachel was careful not to let the rush of pity she felt show in her face or countenance. "And you must be—?"

"Her granny. I got me a Christian name, like everybody else, but you don't need to know it."

"But you look after Christabel?"

"Christabel looks after herself. Sometimes me, too, when my rhumetiz kicks up. Anyways, she ain't got no yen nor need for schoolin', so you jest git back on that old nag and point yerself toward home, wherever that might be."

By now, Rachel's irritation had given way to an interest and amusement she wouldn't have dared to reveal. "I'd still like to speak with Christabel herself, if possible."

As dry and brittle looking as an old grasshopper, Granny Johnson spat again, a stream of what appeared to be tobacco juice this time, into the dooryard, scattering a flock of ropy chickens in every direction. She had yet to lower the shotgun. "It ain't possible. Now, git."

Just then, the cabin door creaked open and a girl about Emma's age hovered on the threshold, squinting against the glare of daylight. She was a plain little creature, with ragged clothes and stringy, unwashed hair of indeterminate color. Even at that distance, the stench from inside that shack struck Rachel hard enough to rock her back on her heels. She hoped her nose hadn't twitched, and pretended to sneeze, just in case.

"Don't go shootin' the schoolmarm, Granny," Christabel said. "You'll bring the law down on us for sure."

Granny spat yet again. Rachel had never known a person who could summon up so much saliva, seemingly at will. "I done told her to git, but she don't seem to hear too well. Tell her you don't want no book learnin' and maybe we'll git shut of her."

Rachel folded her arms. "Is what your grandmother says true, Christabel? Wouldn't you like to learn to read and write and speak like a lady?"

The yearning in Christabel's dirt-smudged face was clear to see, and it squeezed hard at Rachel's heart. "What use would that be?" she asked. "Ain't no books out here. Nobody but Granny to speak to."

Rachel gestured toward the timbered country falling away behind and around them. "There's a whole world out there, Christabel, and a lot of it is pretty wonderful. An education can take you places."

Again, it showed in Christabel's expression and every line of her body, that desperate yearning to be so much more than she was, have so much more than she had. In the end, though, she merely shrugged. "Who'd tend to Granny if I went galivantin' off somewheres?"

Granny said nothing, and she even lowered the shotgun, though the stock made a sharp thumping sound where it struck the warped boards of the porch.

Rachel drew a deep breath and plunged. "With all

due respect," she said evenly, "your Granny won't live forever. And even if you stay right here until the end of your days, if you just go to school, you'll have books to keep you company ever after."

"Don't need no books," Granny grumbled. "We got by jest fine without 'em all this long while."

Christabel took a step forward, her gait awkward because of her twisted right foot. The child was a bed-wetter, that could be told from the miasma surrounding her, but the knowledge only made Rachel all the more determined to rope her in. Of all the pupils who might come within her charge, with the possible exception of Toby Houghton, this one was most in need of her attention and care.

"I could learn to read?" Christabel asked, in a tone of muted wonder.

"Folks would jest laugh at you," Granny put in, helpful to the last. "They'd call names, too."

Rachel bristled. "No one will laugh, unless they've a mind to pass the rest of the day with their nose stuck in a corner. Name-callers will meet with the same fate."

Christabel limped another step forward. "I ain't got a decent dress to wear," she said. "No shoes, neither. Come winter, it'll be a long cold walk down this here hill to Springwater."

Rachel had brought a few yard-goods with her from Pennsylvania, and she suspected that her Sunday shoes might come close enough to fitting Christabel. She and June-bug could put their heads together and come up with a way to get the child into a tub of hot water. Plenty of soaking and scrubbing and combing would do wonders. "I'll sew a dress for you myself," Rachel said, with resolution and reckless optimism, "and I've got an extra pair of shoes."

"We don't take no charity," Granny put in. Her berry-bright eyes were snapping, and her scrawny hands looked fidgety where she held the shotgun, as though she'd like to raise it up again, and draw a bead on the center of Rachel's forehead.

Christabel made her way down the single step and hobbled slowly toward Rachel, her moon-shaped face revealing a careful, tentative hope. "It ain't charity, Granny," she said, without looking back at the old woman or pausing, though it seemed to Rachel that walking on such a foot must be painful. "Not if I make it up in work. I can scrub floors and windows, Miss Rachel, and sweep, too. I can round up stray cows and saddle mules and pitch hay. Ain't much of anything, work-wise, that I don't know how to do. I'd admire to come to school, if there's a way I can make it right to you."

Up close, the odor of that poor child was enough to make Rachel's eyes burn and water. She did not react, however, but simply laid a hand on the girl's shoulder, trusting in the Lord, June-bug McCaffrey, and her own devices to make Christabel presentable. "Lessons begin the last Monday in August," she said. "Do you have a calendar?"

"Don't need one," Christabel said, with the first glimmer of a smile. It changed her plain appearance quite dramatically, that smile. "Granny and me, we

can tell what day it is by the signs." At Rachel's
puzzled expression, she added, "You know, the rings
around the moon and the color of moss and the like.
We mark it off on a bit of paper."

Rachel, while still nearly overwhelmed by the
pervasive stench, felt a sudden desire to embrace the
girl. Would have done so, in fact, if she hadn't been so
innately conscious of Christabel's fragile pride. "I'll be
watching for you," she said. "You come to the
Springwater station, a few days before school starts. In
the meantime, I need to take some kind of measure if
I'm going to make that dress." No need to mention
her private doubts concerning her sewing skills and
discourage everyone.

In the end, they used string, unwillingly fetched by
a sullen Granny, and Rachel took Christabel's meas-
urements, cutting a separate length for each. Then,
sensing that Granny's patience had worn dangerously
thin, Rachel said her farewells, extracted another
assurance of attendance from Christabel, and
mounted her horse.

She waited until she was well out of sight of the
Johnson shack before giving way to tears of sorrow,
frustration, and pity.

Midway down the mountainside, with the smoke of
June-bug's cookstove chimney curling visibly against
the pale blue of the sky, Sunflower came up lame.
Rachel dismounted and raised the mare's left foreleg
to examine the hoof, and sure enough, there was a
raw place in the fleshy portion, though she couldn't
tell whether a shard of glass had gotten inside or not.

"Poor darling," Rachel said, and patted the animal's neck. Then she proceeded toward home, on foot, moving slowly and leading Sunflower by the reins. Jacob could treat the mare's wound, she was certain, but in the interim there was no choice but to keep going.

It was sunset when they reached the edge of the timber and lamps were burning in the windows of the station. There were a dozen horses out in front of the Brimstone Saloon, and it sounded as if a brawl was taking place inside.

Worried about Emma—or so she told herself at the time—Rachel left Sunflower's reins dangling at the side of the road and clomped up onto the wooden step in front of the saloon to peer in over the swinging doors.

Trey sat, hatless, with the sleeves of his white gambler's shirt rolled up and a cheroot clamped between his teeth, at a small table in the center of the room. Seated across from him was a man roughly the size of a one-hole privy, and the two of them were engaged in an arm-wrestling match. The noise came from the half-moon of spectators who looked on from the rear, thereby affording Rachel an unobstructed view. Emma sat on the stairs, watching through the lathe-turned rails, her chin propped in one palm.

Rachel might have gone on about her business if it hadn't been for the sight of that child. Even though Emma didn't look at all disturbed, but merely interested in the proceedings below stairs, the scene, coupled with all she had witnessed on the mountain, brought out the crusader in Rachel. Full of reckless indignation, she shoved the swinging doors open with both hands and stormed into the Brimstone Saloon like a blue norther.

Trey was obviously startled at the sight of her, and relaxed his arm just enough to allow his opponent to slam his hand down onto the tabletop and win the match. Cheers went up all around—except from Trey, of course, who was flushed to the hairline and looked as though he could chew up a stove poker. The winner and his supporters shouted for whiskey, at the same time watching Rachel's steam-engine approach with expressions of eager dread.

Trey rose slowly to his feet to face her. "What the devil—?" he sputtered. Then, evidently too angry to speak, he fell silent. His fists clenched and unclenched at his sides.

Rachel could not have cared less that she'd spoiled the foolish competition for him; she was only worried about the child watching, wide-eyed now, and plainly breathless, from the stairway. Emma gripped a rail in each hand and seemed to be attempting to press her face between them.

Now that she had braved the lion's den, Rachel wasn't entirely certain what she should say or do. She'd entered the Brimstone on the power of an indignant impulse, but some of the locomotion went out of her when she came to stand before Trey, looking up into those furious silver eyes.

She fell back on bravado. "Are you aware," she demanded, in a fierce undertone, "that your daughter has witnessed this entire sorry spectacle?"

Trey raised an eyebrow. He looked slightly calmer, though his eyes were still flashing with sparks. "Which one is worse, Miss English?" he shot back. "That spectacle—or this one?"

Rachel was chagrined because, damn him, he had a point, but she wasn't about to back down. Not in front of Emma and all those seedy drovers. "If you care one whit for that child, you'll send these drunkards away and put an end to this vice once and for all!"

Trey too had his hands on his hips now, and he was leaning in, so that his face was uncomfortably close to Rachel's. "If I close this place down," he retorted, in measured tones, "*that child* will go hungry. Thanks to you, I just lost the first arm-wrestling match of my life, and a five-dollar gold piece along with it!"

Rachel wet her lips with a hasty pass of the tip of her tongue. "Perhaps, then," she responded, "you will think twice before wagering such a sum on a scurrilous contest again!"

One of the onlookers laughed. "This mean you ain't gonna take part in the horse race come Sunday afternoon, Trey?"

Trey silenced the man with a wave of one hand, never so much as looking away from Rachel's face. She felt pinned, even entranced, unable to go forward or backward until he deigned to free her, and that made her angry as a swarm of bees whipped to a frenzy in a butter-churn.

"What horse race?" she demanded.

"The one I mean to win," Trey growled.

"There's a race after Jacob's preachin' and the picnic this comin' Sunday," put in some intrepid and interminably helpful observer, from the humming void that surrounded her and Trey.

Rachel frowned, confused. "A picnic? I hadn't heard about that."

"That," drawled Trey, "is because it was supposed to be a surprise, it being in your honor and all. Miss June-bug's been planning it ever since you agreed to come out here and save us all from our sin and ignorance."

Rachel blushed, and only partly because of the forthcoming picnic that was supposed to be a surprise. She looked around self-consciously, but carefully avoided meeting Emma's gaze, though she felt it like a beam of strong sunlight, full of curiosity and confusion. "I don't know what to say," she said.

"How about 'good-bye'?" Trey asked. "We're conducting business here, in case that's escaped you." He raised a pointer finger and dared—*dared* to waggle it in her face. "Furthermore, Miss English, I plan on winning that race. I've got a sizable amount of money riding on it. See that you don't go interfering again, because if you do, I will not take kindly to it."

Rachel opened her mouth, closed it again, completely at a loss. He was just lucky, she told herself, as cold comfort, that she hadn't bitten his finger off at the middle joint. "My horse is lame," she said, in a corresponding tone of voice. "She needs tending."

Having so spoken, she turned, with all the dignity she could muster, and walked out of the Brimstone Saloon with her chin high. It was only when she got outside, her head spinning with a welter of confusing emotions, none of which could be fitted with a particular name, that she dropped the facade.

The confrontation with Trey Hargreaves had not been an amicable one, and yet she was filled with a strange, tentative sense of celebration, quite unlike anything she'd ever felt before. Underlying this was a dark and utter despair that brought an ache to her heart and tears to the backs of her eyes. On the one hand, she wanted to dance in the street, but her desire to fling herself down on the nearest piece of flat ground and cry herself blind was equally strong.

She tried to remember, as she walked toward Springwater station through a purple twilight, so busy with her thoughts that she was barely aware of her surroundings, poor Sunflower ambling along behind her, whether Langdon had roused such conflicting reactions in her. He hadn't, she concluded; this was all new, and at once as frightening as meeting a grizzly bear in the woods and as splendid as dancing with an angel.

June-bug was seated in her rocker, near the empty hearth, her sewing in her lap. The needle in her hand flashed silver as she worked, but when she looked up and saw Rachel standing in the doorway, she left off her stitching. "My heavens," she said, "what's happened to you?"

Jacob, smoking a pipe next to an open window,

regarded Rachel in thoughtful silence. In their own way, Jacob's silences were as eloquent as the words of any bard.

Rachel remembered that the door was open behind her, letting in flies, and closed it with a groping motion of one hand. "Sunflower's got a sore foot," she said to the stationmaster, sounding strange and helpless even to herself, as though someone else had spoken through her vocal chords. "There was broken glass—I'm afraid she might have picked up a piece or bruised herself somehow, the way she's limping."

Jacob nodded and crossed to the fireplace, tapped his pipe against one wall of the hearth, placing it neatly on the mantel, and went out to see to the injured horse. Toby was already there beside him; Rachel heard his excited voice even through the shut door.

"I believe I asked you a question, young lady," June-bug said, with pointed good humor and a gentleness that made Rachel want to fall into the other woman's arms and wail like a distraught child.

"Something terrible has happened," Rachel said, slowly pacing the length of the long room now, hugging herself as she walked. "Something utterly unexpected and all wrong."

June-bug didn't prod; she simply waited, placid and steady, another shirt for Toby lying half finished in her lap.

"I think—" Rachel lowered her voice, "I think I . . . *care* for Trey Hargreaves."

The vivid blue eyes smiled, even though June-bug's

mouth merely twitched. "No!" she said, in a tone of mock horror.

Rachel came to an abrupt stop in the middle of the room, hugging herself even more tightly than before. "You don't understand. He's all wrong for me, and I'm all wrong for him."

"I see," June-bug said, with a solemn nod.

"He's . . . he's a saloon-keeper!" Rachel cried.

"Yes'um, that's so."

"And I'm a teacher!"

"I reckon you are indeed."

"He hates me!"

"I don't believe that," June-bug said, with the first real conviction she'd shown since the conversation began. "The pair of you have been strikin' sparks since the first day, when Trey fished you out of that bogged-down stagecoach and helped Guffy get the rig to shore. Some of the best matches start that way, with fireworks and plenty of 'em. Why, me and Jacob, we like to have stripped each other's hide right off afore we figured out that we was courtin'."

Rachel covered her face with both hands. "Why? Oh, why?"

"No sense in askin' that," June-bug said wisely. "Ain't no earthly answer, when it comes to such matters."

Rachel peeked between splayed fingers, not quite ready to face the world. June-bug was sewing again, at a quick, contented pace. "I shouldn't have come here."

"Nonsense," June-bug replied, without looking up from the green cotton fabric of Toby's new shirt. "The children need you. And so does Trey. One of these days, he'll reason it through and come a-courtin' proper-like, with flowers and pretty words."

The image made Rachel laugh out loud. It was as incongruous as—well, as Trey at a tea party, sipping from a delicate china cup and nibbling at a molasses-oatmeal cookie. "Even if he did—which is about as likely as St. Peter coming in on the next stagecoach— I couldn't marry him. Our principles and values are at variance to say the least, and besides, I will never give up teaching."

"Hmmm," said June-bug, rocking and stitching.

Rachel slumped onto a nearby bench and leaned back against the table's edge, suddenly spent. She had to change the subject, or lose her sanity. "I visited Christabel Johnson today," she said.

June-bug nodded. "You told me you was a-goin' to."

"Granny offered to shoot me—in case I was tired of living, I guess."

At that, the stationmistress chuckled. "That's Granny. She's nobody to trifle with. Why, one time some cowboys got drunked up—just kids really, passin' through and meanin' no real harm—and went up there with a mind to tip over Granny's outhouse. She put so much buckshot in them boys that it took Jacob and me half the next day to pick out the lead." She winced a little at the memory, shook her head and chuckled again.

"Naturally," Rachel said, simply not up to dealing with the image of a lot of cowboys with their drawers pulled down for the procedure, "it's Christabel I'm concerned with. I think I've persuaded her to come to school when classes begin, but there are a couple of problems. She has no clothes or shoes to speak of, but I can make her a dress or two from the yard goods I brought and give her my extra shoes. She'll still need a coat, though, and then there's the sorry state of her hygiene."

June-bug made a *tsk-tsk* sound with her tongue. "That poor little snippet," she said. "You just bring her to me, and I'll get her bathed. Maybe I can move Granny to let her board here, just through the winter."

"I don't think the old woman will agree to that," Rachel replied, with a sigh. "She says she needs the girl to help around the place, and it's probably true."

"Bullfeathers," said June-bug. That was as close as she ever came to cursing in all the time Rachel knew her. "Granny Johnson ain't helpless. She's just got that little girl buffaloed, that's all. I'm going to hitch up the buggy and drive up there and pay her a call first chance I git. Maybe tomorrow morning, in fact, if the stage comes in on time and I can get everybody fed afore it's time to start supper."

If anyone could reason with Granny, June-bug could. Rachel's spirits, chafed raw by the events of the day, rose a little. "I'll see to tomorrow's supper," she said. "You see to that incorrigible old lady."

"Fair enough," June-bug agreed, with a small smile. "I don't reckon Granny'll shoot at me, but you never know."

Rachel headed for her room, there to wash, change her clothes, brush out her hair, and pin it up again. Attending to her personal grooming invariably made her feel better, and the delicious scent of something roasting in the oven had gone a long way toward restoring her as well.

The cleanliness remedy did not fail her; when she returned to the main room, Jacob and Toby were back, standing side by side, scrubbing their hands and faces at the washstand. Toby looked at Rachel with a light in his eyes.

"Sunflower's gonna be all right, Miss English. It was just a little scratch. We cleaned it good and put on some medicine. Jacob put her out to graze in the pasture for a while, so she'll get a chance to heal up."

Jacob merely smiled and placed a big hand on the boy's shoulder, in silent verification of his words. Somehow, it seemed like more, that simple gesture, a confirmation of Toby's very being, the masculine blessing Mike Houghton either could not or would not give.

"That's wonderful, Toby," Rachel said, dropping her gaze from Jacob's face to the lad's. "Perhaps you'll grow up to be an animal doctor."

"I want to run a stagecoach station, like Jacob," the boy said, with a shake of his head and a look of determination.

"Might not be much call for that, with the railroads comin' on the way they are," Jacob observed, but Toby was undaunted.

"I ain't leavin' Springwater," he said. "Not even if my pa comes back meanin' to fetch me."

At that, Rachel and Jacob exchanged another look. If indeed Mike Houghton returned, he could reclaim his boy and there would be nothing anyone could do to prevent him, and they both knew it. The fact that Houghton neglected and probably abused his son meant little in the eyes of the law; children, like women and dogs, had only the most minimal rights.

Jacob squeezed Toby's narrow shoulder. "I reckon we'd better deal with that when and if it happens," he said. "In the meanwhile, we'll just do the best we can. How's that?"

Toby turned and looked up at the older man with something resembling adoration. "That's just fine," he said, in complete trust.

The following morning, the stage arrived right on time, and the three passengers alighted to stretch their legs, take hot meals, and attend to other personal needs. All of them were moving on, and as soon as the coach was loaded up again, June-bug removed her apron and handed it to Rachel.

"Jacob," June-bug said, "I'll need the buggy and a shotgun. I'm goin' up the mountain to pay a call on Granny Johnson."

"You mean to shoot her?" Jacob asked, with the merest twitch at the corner of his mouth.

"I don't require no shotgun to deal with Granny. If'n I were to meet up with a mama grizzly, well, that would be somethin' different entirely."

"Maybe I ought to go with you," Jacob said, looking uncertain.

June-bug shook her head. "You've got that worn-out team of horses to feed and water and rub down," she said, referring to the eight animals that had drawn the stage west to Springwater, from over Choteau way. As always, Jacob and the driver had hitched fresh horses to the coach and led the tired ones away to the stable. "You see to them poor critters. Rachel's goin' to wash up the dishes, sweep the floor, and start supper for me."

Jacob raised his eyebrows at that, though he offered no comment. It was unusual for June-bug to let anyone take over the tasks she saw as hers to do, and one didn't have to be married to her for forty-odd years, like Jacob, to know that.

"I'd better take along a few of them cookies," June-bug mused, bustling toward the pantry. "Some eggs and butter, too, I think. I know they ain't got no cow up there, and with winter just past, them chickens of theirs are probably as scrawny-lookin' as Granny herself."

Rachel couldn't help laughing a little. June-bug had a pretty good handle on Granny Johnson and her environs, for someone who claimed not to know her well. Clearing up and sweeping was good therapy for Rachel, and she was humming under her breath by the time June-bug set out for the little shack tilting up there on the mountainside, like a climber hanging on for dear life.

"Maybe I should have gone along to protect Miss June-bug from Injuns and the like," Toby said, watching from the front window.

Jacob had resumed his pipe-smoking on the opposite side of the room. "Don't you fret," he said, with a twinkle in his dark eyes. "If it comes down to a squabble, it'll be the Indians that need protectin', not Miss June-bug."

Jacob's trust in his bride was well-placed, as it turned out. Four hours later, the buggy clattered back into the dooryard and there was Miss June-bug, safe and sound, with a wide-eyed Christabel bouncing on the seat beside her.

CHAPTER

6

TOBY LOOKED Christabel up and down, squeezed his nostrils shut with a thumb and two fingers, and keened, "Phew! You stink bad as an outhouse!"

"That will be enough," Jacob said gravely, from behind the boy. They were all three standing outside the station entrance, Rachel and Jacob and Toby.

Miss June-bug waggled a finger at the lad. "You jest git yourself into your room, Toby Houghton, and work out why it was wrong to say a thing like that. When you've got it clear in your head, you'll be ready to apologize to Christabel."

Toby looked up at Jacob, as if expecting intercession, but the man only gestured toward the house and ground out, "Go."

Flushed and probably already repentant, if unprepared to say as much, Toby took his leave.

"Who's that?" Christabel inquired, looking to Rachel as though she might bolt and flee back into the hills. Her eyes accused, *You said nobody would be mean to me. You promised.*

"His name is Toby Houghton," Rachel said. "Don't you worry about him. He's a good boy, and he'll turn out to be your friend, you just wait and see."

Christabel looked doubtful; she'd most likely never had a friend, unless you counted her grandmother. "I don't reckon I do smell much like town-folk do," she said sorrowfully.

"We'll attend to your bath straight away," Miss June-bug said, as though proposing that a guest take a bath were the same as offering tea or a place in the shade on a hot day. "I believe I've got some things you could wear while Miss English here is stitching up a dress or two."

Rachel had not even begun the sewing project, as she hadn't expected June-bug to succeed so quickly in her mission of bringing Christabel Johnson down from the mountainside. She was anxious, even excited, to proceed, despite her dubious abilities as a seamstress. Her heart swelled as she put an arm around the young girl; she knew well what courage it had taken for her to break away from familiar miseries and step into an uncertain future.

They set up the big washtub out in the high grass behind the station, and Jacob, June-bug, and Rachel all carried hot water until it was brimming. The job of scrubbing Christabel from head to foot fell to the women, of course, and when it was over, both Rachel and June-bug were as wet as their beaming charge.

When at last Christabel's hair was clean enough to

suit June-bug—a tendril of it had to "squeak" between her fingers at a gentle tug—they helped her out of the big tub and wrapped her in a blanket, to keep her from taking a chill. It was sunset by then, and everyone was thinking in terms of supper, a pot of baked beans Rachel had put into the oven earlier that day, to be accompanied by slices of leftover cornbread and some canned carrots from the pantry.

Christabel ate as though she'd never tasted such food before; maybe she hadn't, given the poverty she and her grandmother lived in. Toby came out of his room behind the stove, looking chagrined, in the middle of the meal.

"I reckon I'm sorry for what I said," he told Christabel, in staunch tones. "It weren't mannerly." He rustled up a game smile, even as his stomach rumbled for all to hear. "'Sides, you cleaned up right nice."

Jacob, June-bug, and Rachel all made a shared effort not to show their amusement, but the sternness of their expressions lacked some element of true conviction.

"Thanks," Christabel said. Her eyes were watchful. Her fine, thin hair, which had turned out to be a pretty shade of brown, gleamed in the lamplight, still moist from washing and ridged from June-bug's comb. Her borrowed dress, oversized but clean, was worn with a certain wary pride. "You better set down and have yourself some of these here beans. They ain't as bad as they look."

Rachel bit her lower lip and did not dare to look at Jacob or June-bug, lest she burst out laughing after all.

Toby peered over the girl's shoulder to inspect Rachel's baked beans. "I reckon you're right," he said, and took the place that had been laid for him, on the other side of the table, next to Jacob. Both children consumed second and then third helpings of the main course, and together they finished off the cornbread.

All and all, it was a companionable meal, though mostly passed in silence.

Christabel's eyes were especially large as she got up from the table at last and reached for her empty plate. "I'll wash up the dishes," she said. "Then I suppose I ought to lay myself down and sleep, since I'm plum tuckered out."

June-bug rose gracefully from her own seat and took the plate out of Christabel's hands. "You'll have your chores to do, that's for sure and certain. But you can start in on them tomorrow."

"I guess I don't know where you mean to put me," Christabel confided, with painful shyness. "I don't see no loft nor pallet nor anything like that."

"Fact is, we do rent out what rooms we've got to travelers, whenever the need arises, but in the meantime, you're welcome to whichever bed you want," June-bug said, laying a hand to the child's thin shoulder. "And don't you fret, neither. We'll make a place where you can stay, permanent-like, if that's what you want to do."

Christabel looked amazed. "A whole room? All to myself?"

June-bug smiled. "Come along, and we'll make up the bed with fresh linens and all." With that, they left the dining room together, June-bug slowing her steps to match Christabel's more labored pace.

Rachel, long since finished eating, got up to clear away and wash dishes, while Jacob and Toby went out to attend to the evening chores. Standing at the work table in the kitchen, gazing out the darkened window, Rachel could see the lights of the Brimstone Saloon, glowing in the darkness. Her thoughts traipsed in that direction, seeking Trey. Finding him all too easily.

Sunday morning, after breakfast and chores, Jacob announced that he felt called to preach a rousing sermon. He put on his good black suit and string tie for the occasion, once the barn work was done, and got out his ancient Bible. It seemed that his very decision to conduct a service had stirred the surrounding countryside to life, though of course Rachel knew that the day had been planned for some time.

The spring sun shone extra-bright, the breeze was fresh, and the wildflowers covered the fields like threads in a colorful patchwork quilt.

With help from Toby and Christabel, Rachel moved the tables to one side of the room and set all the benches in tidy rows, facing the fireplace, for June-bug said that Jacob liked to do his preaching in front of the hearth. He'd acquired the habit over the course of several Montana winters, she confided, when the whole territory turned to ice and crystal.

June-bug herself was occupied with frying up chicken and boiling potatoes and eggs for a massive salad.

Slowly, as noon approached, Jacob's parishioners began to appear—Landry Kildare and his two boys, both void of war paint and with their hair combed down, were the first to arrive, then came the Bell-weathers, followed by a few old bachelor traders, all of whom looked as though they hadn't been out of the woods in twenty years. They were all shy, these mountain men, but their eagerness to be part of the gathering showed plainly in their eyes. There were cowboys, too, spruced up and on their best behavior, passing through Springwater in advance of one of several large herds of cattle being driven up from Denver and points further south. Rachel recognized some of them from the arm-wrestling contest at Brimstone Saloon, though she had to admit they didn't look like the same fellows at all, with their clean hair and stiffly new dungarees.

Emma Hargreaves came in, somewhat timidly, wearing a bright yellow Sunday-go-to-meeting dress that fit her, unlike the borrowed garb Christabel had on, and the Kildare boys' of nearly outgrown trousers and button-stretched shirts. Kathleen Bellweather ran to greet Emma, being about the same age, though she had given Christabel a wide berth, and Rachel held herself back from stepping in. If she pressed the children to be friends, she knew, she might well create a permanent breach between them, but it was hard not to intercede all the same.

The noisy arrival of a buckboard drew her attention

away from the children, and she gave a gasp of joy when she looked through a front window and saw the Wainwright family, all dressed up and ready for preaching and a party. Rachel ran outside to greet them, and embraced first Abigail, then Evangeline. Scully was holding the baby in the crook of one arm and little J.J. in the other, grinning at his wife's delight.

"I didn't dare to hope you would come all this way!" Rachel cried, holding Evangeline by the shoulders.

Evangeline smiled. "We wouldn't have missed it. Besides, Scully wants to see the horse race."

Rachel was reminded of Trey Hargreaves, and she felt a mild ache in the depths of her heart. There was no sign of him, and if they met, they were likely to have words, but still she kept watching for him, at the edge of her vision. "You don't plan to enter?" she asked Scully, reaching out for the well-bundled baby. He surrendered the child and used both arms to keep a fidgety J.J. in check. "I should think that Appaloosa of yours could run like the wind."

"He can," Scully said, with a mischievous light in his eyes, "but I'm an old married man now, and henpecked into the bargain. My dear wife is of the opinion that I spend enough time in the saddle as it is, owing to my profession, without making a sport of it."

Before Rachel could shape a reply, June-bug erupted from the station doorway, both arms extended.

"Let me see that baby this minute!" she demanded joyously.

Evangeline laughed, as did Rachel, who surrendered little Rachel Louisa into her friend's embrace. The blue sky seemed to cast a blessing over them all, and there was laughter and conviviality spilling out of the station itself, ambrosia to the spirit.

"Oh," cried June-bug, having unveiled the baby from her blanket, "she is the *loveliest* little thing—fair as an angel!"

It was merely what people routinely said about new babies, but in this case, it was also the purest truth. The Wainwright infant was pretty as the cherubs in the paintings of the Old Masters, and Rachel was certain she would grow up to be a legendary beauty. Evangeline thanked June-bug for the compliment with a certain pleased modesty, and they all went inside to settle down for Jacob's sermon.

He'd chosen the 91st Psalm as his text, and he was indeed a gifted orator, but Rachel only heard about half of his message because Trey Hargreaves slipped in, midway through the rustic service, to take a chair at the back of the room, next to the door, the benches being full.

Rachel had glanced back when she heard the hinges creak and caught sight of him. From that moment on, her concentration was shattered and she could think of nothing but Trey. In the brief look she'd taken, she'd seen that he was wearing a nicely fitted suit of clothes, with one of his white ruffled shirts and a well-shined pair of boots; his dark hair was clean and brushed, and he'd shaved for the occasion as well.

When the preaching ended, after some two hours, everyone was ready to stand outside under the two shade trees, the women fanning themselves, the men talking of horses and cattle and the weather. All the ladies had brought food to contribute, and there was plenty to set out on the long tables inside, now moved back to their proper places. June-bug was in her element, overseeing it all, just as her husband had been earlier, when he stood before his motley congregation, Bible in hand, deep voice ringing with conviction.

The children, relieved to be released from their injunction to sit quietly, raced all around the station, shouting and laughing. Only Christabel was left out, perched quietly on the edge of a chair someone had brought out and set in the shade of the building, watching the happy foolery with carefully expressionless eyes.

Rachel was about to break her own rule and have a word with the others about including Christabel in their games, when she saw Trey, standing in a circle of men, reach out and snag his daughter as she ran past. He bent and spoke to her, nodding subtly in Christabel's direction.

Rachel stood still, watching, as Emma walked slowly over to Christabel's chair and spoke to her. Christabel smiled, then shook her head and ducked her face shyly.

Emma took hold of her arm and tugged, and soon, miraculously, Christabel was a part of things, if still somewhat on the fringe of it all. Given her crippled foot, it was nearly impossible for her to keep up, but she tried valiantly, and Emma often stopped and came back to encourage her.

Rachel closed her eyes for a moment, so moved that she did not think she could have spoken, had there been anyone at hand to speak to, that is.

As it happened, there was someone close by. Trey Hargreaves had materialized at her elbow, hat in hand.

Rachel blinked, taken by surprise. "Mr. Hargreaves," she said, somewhat squeakily, by way of a greeting.

He nodded. "Afternoon," he said. There was a grin lurking behind that serious expression of his, and though he was making a fine job of holding it in restraint, now and again it peeked out of his eyes. "There'll be dancing tonight," he informed her. "Old Zeb Prudham brought his fiddle."

Rachel's heart beat a little faster, though she couldn't think why that should happen. Heaven knew, she'd certainly danced—though not since Langdon went away to war, of course. If she were called upon to participate in the festivities, she'd manage to keep from tangling her feet. "Yes?" she said.

She thought she saw the faintest flush of color under Trey's tan, but she couldn't be sure. "I reckon every man here is going to want a whirl around the floor with you," he said, and it looked as though every word was costing him dearly. "For the sake of peace between us, you understand, well—" He looked away, looked back determinedly. "I'd like to be the first. To dance with you, I mean."

Rachel was taken aback by the request, mightily so. Of all the men in and around Springwater, Trey was the last one she would have expected to approach her with such a request. She wasn't exactly his kind of woman, was she? Her heartbeat stepped up again.

"I'd like that," she said, with no more grace than the average smitten schoolgirl.

Trey tilted his head toward her and spoke in a confidential fashion. "Just between you and me, I think that Kildare feller means to court you for a wife. He's good-looking, I guess, and he's got himself a good piece of land and some fine horseflesh. Solvent, too—he's been trying to buy my old homestead up behind his place for a year. Offering cash, too." He paused and frowned, as though aware that he might be making his friend look too good. "You hitch up with him, though, and those kids of his will have you in an asylum before a year's out."

Rachel wanted to laugh, out of nervousness and exultation, but she controlled the urge. "I see," she said. "I'll bear that in mind."

"Good," Trey replied, in earnest satisfaction and what appeared to be a measure of relief.

Before the conversation could proceed, June-bug informed the gathering that the midday meal was a-wasting and they'd better come inside and help themselves before the flies got it all. The response was enthusiastic, but Jacob lead a short, rumbling prayer before the first fork was raised.

Rachel had the fanciful feeling that she was in the midst of a homecoming; it was as if she'd belonged in Springwater all along, without knowing of its existence, and had at last found her way there, having traveled over a long and winding path.

The meal was delicious, a rousing affair, during which Granny Johnson caused a stir by arriving on the back of a brown mule, wearing a calico bonnet with her old dress and carrying the ever-present shotgun across her lap. "Did I miss the preachin'?" she asked, when Jacob helped her down off the animal's back.

"Yes, Ma'am," Jacob answered soberly, "you did at that."

"Dern it," Granny said. "I ain't heard a good sermon in twenty years. I had my brain all set for fire and brimstone."

Jacob's mouth twitched, but he had the good grace not to smile. While he'd certainly driven home the power of the Lord in his message, he hadn't stirred the embers of hell into a roaring blaze, the way a lot of preachers did. Privately, Rachel thought better of him for it, although she knew that many people didn't count themselves forgiven if they hadn't felt the sharp prongs of the devil's pitchfork.

Now, he stood with his hand resting lightly, in a gentlemanly fashion, on the small of Granny's back. "There's still a good bit of food left, Mrs. Johnson," he said. "You go right on in there and fill yourself a plate."

Granny nodded and handed him the shotgun. "If you'll look after that for me, young feller, I'll be obliged," she said. Then she tottered toward the door of the station, stopping briefly to speak to Rachel. "I jest came here to see how you're treatin' my gal," she announced. "If she ain't happy, I'm takin' her right home agin."

Rachel smiled. She was pleased to see Granny attending the festivities, testy though she was. It had troubled her not a little to think of the old woman out there in that shack, all alone, and she dared to hope Granny might actually become a part of the community. Not only would that make the elderly lady's life easier, but it would be a boon to Christabel, too.

Soon, Rachel spotted the two of them, side by side on a sawhorse, Granny with a plateful of fried chicken, potato salad, and pickles in her lap, Christabel chattering earnestly and gesturing with one hand. Rachel smiled and sought out Evangeline, who wanted a look at the inside of the schoolhouse.

By the time they returned from that, the horse race was about to begin. The course was to cover the stagecoach trail from the station to Willow Creek and back, and everybody was on their honor not to take any shortcuts. The prize was a twenty-dollar gold piece, raised by the entrance fees, and there were seven contestants, including Trey, horses prancing at the rope Jacob had laid across the road to form both the starting line and the finish.

The rules were announced—no kicking, punching, or spurring of other riders, and no cutting across the meadow. Cursing was allowed, since there were no ladies entered in the race, and spitting was all right, too. If any fights broke out, everybody concerned would get themselves disqualified.

Having stated all this, Jacob raised his pistol into the air and fired. The racers took off, streaks of man and horseflesh, pounding toward the first bend, raising dust. Rachel was secretly pleased to see that Trey was already in the lead, but it wouldn't have been diplomatic for the schoolmarm to single out one rider over the others, so she just watched until they'd all disappeared from sight. Toby and the Kildare boys chased across the meadow, to keep the horses in view, all of them yearning, no doubt, for the day when they might ride in such a race as well.

It was several miles to the creek and back, but the excitement of the spectators was not dimmed by the fact that the horses and their riders would be out of sight for a long time. There weren't many such gatherings in that isolated place, so this was high adventure for most everyone there, especially the children.

Nearly forty-five minutes later, the first rider reappeared, far ahead of the others, and Rachel had a hard time keeping herself from jumping up and down when she saw that it was Trey. When he shot across the finish line, his horse barely winded, cheers went up and loud congratulations were offered. Had it been any day but Sunday, Rachel thought, most of the men would probably have adjourned to the Brimstone for a celebratory glass of whiskey.

Amid the handshakes and back slaps, Trey looked up, found Rachel, and winked. It was an outlandish thing to do, sure to start talk, but she was pleased all the same.

Through the afternoon, the men played horseshoes and the women gossiped at one of June-bug's tables, inside the station, while the smaller children napped on various beds and other acceptable surfaces about the place. The older children seemed to have inexhaustible supplies of energy, and played outdoor games that kept them busy until sunset, when the lamps were lit and the food was brought out again. These were the leftovers from dinner, and yet, like the loaves and fishes in the Bible, there was plenty for everybody, with some to spare.

When the meal ended, the women cleared away and washed the dishes. Each family had brought their own plates, cups, and utensils, as well as something to add to the meal itself. The men moved the tables again, this time out into the dooryard, where a crisp spring breeze was blowing, to make room inside for dancing.

Zeb Prudham brought out his fiddle and took up a place before the fire, where a cheerful blaze was crackling, making a great show of tuning each string to within a hair of the note. His antics were, Rachel knew, an integral part of the merrymaking, and she enjoyed them wholeheartedly.

As they had agreed, Trey, who had been keeping his distance since winning the horse race, strode across the room to claim the first dance. As he swept her into his arms, Rachel caught a glimpse of Evangeline's beaming smile, but her attention was soon firmly fastened on Trey and only Trey. She could not seem to look away from his face, and after a while they might have been alone in that large room, for all the notice they spared for anyone else.

Rachel was blushing when the song, the sorrowful ballad *Lorena*, at last came to an end. Being held so close to Trey had had a very strange and flustering effect on her; she felt as though she would surely faint if she didn't get some fresh air. The whole of her person was a single, thrumming ache, and the blood rushed through her veins to set every nerve to pulsing.

The night was deliciously cool, and the stars were out in legions, though the moon was but a sliver. Rachel walked rapidly, fluttering one hand in front of her face in lieu of a fan, and wondering what precisely she was going to do. She was wildly, desperately attracted to Trey Hargreaves, that much was obvious, but she couldn't have made a poorer choice if she'd tried. Men like him didn't marry and settle down to raise families—Emma had probably been an accident. He might want Rachel—he might want a lot of women—but when the conquest was made, he would tire of her and move on.

She was thinking these troubling thoughts, and dashing unconsciously at her cheeks with the back of one hand, when she realized she was nearly to the schoolhouse, and someone was behind her. She turned, hoping to see Evangeline, or perhaps one of the McCaffreys, but instead, there was Trey.

He fell into step beside her. "That was a fine dance,

Miss English," he said. "Thank you for doing me the honor."

She turned, fists clenched, and glared up at him. "Why are you doing this?" she cried.

"Doing what?" he asked, and though he sounded puzzled, she could see by his expression that he knew precisely what she was talking about.

Rachel sent her arms wheeling out, wide of her body. "Being nice to me!" she snapped. "Just yesterday we were shouting at each other!"

"I think we're shouting at each other now," he pointed out reasonably, but he didn't raise his voice, and his eyes were full of gentle humor. "Well, *you're* shouting," he clarified.

They were standing in the middle of what everyone hoped would someday be a street, though at the time it was merely a cattle trail. Rachel shook her finger under his nose. "Maybe I'm not a virgin," she hissed, "but I am no loose woman!"

Trey furrowed his brow, but the humor was still dancing in his eyes. "You're not a virgin?" he echoed. "Teacher! That's a scandal."

Rachel was mortified; she could not believe she'd said such a thing, and yet she had. Heaven help her, she had. Well, maybe that would solve the whole problem. Maybe now that he knew she wasn't pure and untouched, he wouldn't want her anymore. Maybe he wouldn't make *her* want *him*.

He took her shoulders in his hands when she would have turned and fled. "Rachel," he said, "listen to me.

Something important is happening here and we'd
damn well better find out what it is before it drives the
pair of us crazy."

She blinked. She'd expected him to spurn her—
most men thought the world ought to contain a
perpetual supply of virgins, and only virgins, for them
to deflower at their discretion, but it did not seem to
bother Trey that she'd been with another man. "We
don't need to know," she blurted. "What's happening, I mean. We can just go on, both of us, and
pretend nothing has changed."

"Maybe you can," Trey said, frowning and giving
her the slightest shake, "but I can't. I have to know."

"But why?"

"This is why," he said, and then he hauled her
close, bent his head, and covered her mouth with his.
Rachel struggled a moment, more against herself than
him, and then sagged against him with a murmur of
bewildered pleasure. He prodded her lips apart and
entered her with his tongue, and the contact was like
trying to climb a pole made out of pure lightning.
Finally, he held her at arm's length again, his silvery
eyes glittering like shards from a broken moon. "I
reckon I have made my point," he said, somewhat
breathlessly.

Rachel was standing there, trying to will some
starch into her knees, one hand splayed across her
bosom to keep her heart from beating its way right out
of her chest and flying off like a bird. "What are we
going to do?" she asked, after a long time.

"I know what I'd *like* to do," Trey said, ruefully,

thrusting a hand through his hair. "But that's out of the question. Fact is, if we don't get back to that dance right now, there's bound to be gossip. That's nothing new for me, but it might be the ruin of you."

Rachel knew he was right, though the last thing she wanted was to walk back into that station and face all those people. She was sure Trey's kiss had set something ablaze inside her that would be visible for miles, let alone in the confines of a fairly crowded room.

He took her hand, very gently, and slipped it into the crook of his elbow. "Come on, Teacher. There's only one way to spare your reputation, and that's to dance with every man who asks you for the rest of the evening."

She nodded, sniffled once, and allowed him to escort her back into the station. The light of the lanterns, dim though it was, seemed blinding after the darkness, and the music stopped the instant they crossed the threshold, though that was surely an accident of fate.

Jacob, ever the gentleman, presented himself immediately and offered a big hand to Rachel. "May I have the honor of this dance, Miss English?" he asked.

Rachel could have kissed him, for as Jacob went, so went the general populace of Springwater and the surrounding environs. She took his hand, nodded, and let him whirl her into a lively reel. Soon, the floor was a-spin with dancers and she lost sight of Trey entirely. Evangeline passed her, in Scully's arms, and even Granny Johnson was kicking up her heels with

one of the mountain men. The girls, Emma and
Abigail, Kathleen and Christabel, danced with each
other, while the boys stood on the sidelines, looking
stubbornly terrified. No doubt they feared being
dragged into the fray by that most dreaded of crea-
tures, a *girl*.

By the end of the evening, when folks began to
gather up children and picnic baskets and start for
home, it seemed that everyone had forgotten how the
new schoolmarm had gone outside alone with the
owner of the Brimstone Saloon, thereby committing
an impropriety that would have gotten a lot of
teachers dismissed from their jobs. Everyone had
forgotten, that is, except for the new schoolmarm
herself.

CHAPTER

7

A WEEK AFTER THE DANCE, Rachel was at the schoolhouse, rearranging the few things there were to rearrange. Emma and Christabel had been helping out all morning, but she had sent them down to the station on an errand, only moments before, when the ground began to tremble and a horrendous roar shook the walls.

Cattle, Rachel realized—apparently, she had been so engrossed in her efforts at organization that she hadn't heard them approaching. Now, the herd thundered into town, accompanied by whooping cowboys firing pistols into the air. Furious, she hurried across the room and flung open the door.

The cacophony was rivaled only by the dust, which veiled the sky and sent gritty gusts of wind rolling over her. The time Rachel had spent outside earlier, teetering on an upturned crate while she washed windows, was all for naught.

Emma and Christabel.

The realization that the children might well have stumbled straight into the melee seized Rachel suddenly, forced the very breath from her lungs. Dashing toward the street, she searched for them, frantic with fear, but she could see nothing, but for the surreal, shadow-like shapes of cattle and horses and cowboys.

She screamed the girls' names, but could barely hear her own voice over the din.

The herd, already frightened and confused, proceeded to panic, and became a great, swirling knot of hoof and horn, virtually filling the small settlement from one end to the other.

Again, Rachel cried out, but by that time she was coughing. Gaining the road, she plunged into the center of the madness, desperate to find the children before they were run down or gored. She felt the heat and brawny substance of the beasts, smelled their rough, dusty hides. She struggled to stay on her feet, but soon enough she was down, surrounded, smothered, blinded.

This was how it would end, then, she thought, with what struck her as a ludicrous sense of equanimity. She would be trampled to death. So much for the old dream of dying in her sleep, ancient of days.

In the next instant, however, she glimpsed a hand reaching down toward her, and out of pure instinct, she reached back. With a wrench so fearsome that she thought her shoulder had been dislocated, she was pulled upward, and found herself on the back of a horse, Trey's horse, specifically, with Trey at the reins, furious and covered in yellow-brown dust.

"The girls!" she gasped, when the shock of being alive subsided a little, looking wildly about, seeing nothing but dirt and cattle and cowboys.

"They're all right," Trey yelled back, over the uproar, expertly guiding the horse through what seemed to Rachel like a medieval battle.

Soon, they were safe in the dooryard of the station. Two sheepish cowboys rode in behind them, but Rachel had eyes only for Christabel and Emma, who were standing at the edge of the road, faces pale and solemn with alarm. Thank God, Rachel thought, thank God. They'd been here all the time, the girls had, with the McCaffreys to look after them.

"We're mighty sorry about the boys carryin' on the way they have," one of the drovers said, to the general assembly, with a tug at the brim of his hat.

Trey's jawline looked as cold, hard, and smooth as creek stone; Rachel wanted to stay just where she was, safe in the circle of his arms, but of course that couldn't happen. He leaned down and set her carefully on the ground, directing his words to the man who had spoken, probably the trail boss.

"They're welcome in my saloon," he said evenly, his silver eyes glinting bright as knife-blades in the sun. "All the same, they damn near killed somebody. You've got a quarter of an hour to settle those jackals down and get the cattle out into the countryside before I get my rifle and start shooting. I won't be too choosy about what I aim at, I warn you."

Nobody doubted that he meant exactly what he was saying, especially Rachel. He was as outraged a man as she'd ever seen, and for the first time since she'd met him, she realized that he was indeed capable of following through with just such a threat.

It chilled her, knowing that. She stared at him, stunned, and he must have sensed that she was watching him, because he met her eyes squarely, and the truth passed, unspoken, between them.

June-bug came forward, *tsk-tsk*ing, while Jacob took a steadying hold on Rachel's arm, for which she was infinitely grateful. As the reality of what had so nearly happened struck her for the second time, her knees turned to water and she probably would have collapsed without her friend's support.

Trey glanced at his daughter, then Rachel again, and reined his horse away, toward the Brimstone. Rachel stood, leaning against Jacob and watching him go. Something broke inside her, a dam of some sort, behind which she'd hidden all her most private and troublesome emotions. Her sorrow over Langdon and her guilt because she could not save her heart for him after all, her long-suppressed yearnings for a husband and a home and children of her own, her ill-advised but unquestionable love for one particular, impossible man. A man who carried a terrible secret. Spinning like flotsam in the onslaught, she turned to Jacob, laid her head on his shoulder, and wept inconsolably.

He just stood there, God bless him, steady as a tree, holding her with one arm and patting her back with the other hand. "Here now," he said, over and over again, "here now." And somehow, it was infinitely comforting, that simple, meaningless phrase.

Within an hour, everyone was composed again— June-bug had taken the girls in hand, soothing and reassuring them in her cheerful fashion, and Rachel had retreated to her room long enough for a sponge bath and a change of clothing. She brushed the dust from her hair, put it back into its customary loose chignon, and marched herself out into the center of things again. She'd feared that if she stayed in that room too long, she might just crawl under the bed and refuse to come out.

"Those tears," June-bug asked gently, pouring tea the instant Rachel reappeared, "what were they all about?" There was no sign of Jacob or Toby, and Emma and Christabel were in the latter's small room, talking excitedly.

Rachel sighed and let her shoulders slump. "I think you could guess," she replied.

"You're in love with Trey Hargreaves," June-bug said, "and you don't think there's any hope of things workin' out for the two of you."

Rachel nodded and sagged onto a bench at the table, heartily grateful for the steaming cupful of fresh tea set before her. She felt strangely fragile, she who had been so strong all her life, so independent, and dangerously near another useless fit of crying. "I've been lying to myself," she confessed miserably. "Saying I didn't need anyone else. But I do, June-bug—I do. I need the wrong man."

June-bug sat down across from her and poured a cup of tea for herself, adding two lumps of coarse sugar and a dollop of milk before she spoke. "Maybe Trey *ain't* the wrong man. That ever occur to you? Maybe he's the right one, put by for you back when the stars was set in their places."

Rachel felt a surge of affection for this dear friend, who spoke in so homey a fashion and was so very wise. She would have liked for June-bug to be right, but she still had grave doubts. "It won't work. I can't live over a saloon—and not because I'm too fancy and think too highly of myself, either. It's because I don't believe such places are good for people. I know without even asking that Trey won't give up his interest in the Brimstone, any more than I'm willing to stop teaching. How can problems like that ever be solved?"

June-bug shrugged, looking placidly confident, and took a sip of her tea. "I reckon you and Trey would have to decide on the solutions between yourselves. Folks have worked through a lot worse, I can tell you that much."

"It seems impossible."

"So do lots of other things that get done every day."

Rachel sighed. "I'm confused," she admitted. "I had the distinct impression that you didn't approve of Trey Hargreaves."

"I don't like that saloon of his, and that's a fact. I don't reckon I'd spit on the place if it took fire. But I've got nothing agin Trey. Fact is, I respect him a lot, for the way he looks after that little girl in there, if nothin' else," June-bug answered, with a nod toward Christabel's closet-sized room. "That says a lot about a man, to my way of thinkin', his bein' willin' to take responsibility for his child. A lot of them don't—like Mike Houghton, for instance. Trey could probably have found another relative to take Emma in, but he didn't. When she needed him, he made a place for her."

Rachel couldn't refute any of that, but then, Trey's morals weren't the cause of her dilemma in the first place. Had he been a different man than the one she'd glimpsed behind that incorrigibly stubborn exterior, she would never have fallen in love with him. No, it was more than the smaller differences that had worried her all along—the saloon and the gambling, her desire to keep teaching. He was going to tell her something about himself, she sensed that, something she didn't want to hear, didn't want to know. She'd seen it in his eyes, out there in the road.

Not unexpectedly, Trey came to call that night and solemnly asked Rachel to go out for a walk with him. Although his expression was grim, he was slicked up like a man headed for his own hanging, and he carried a bunch of wildflowers, obviously just gathered, in one hand.

She accepted the blossoms with a certain poignant sorrow and put them in water, after quietly accepting his invitation. She borrowed a shawl from June-bug before leaving the station, for the breeze was crisp, despite the fact that summer would be soon be upon them.

"You must know that I care about you," Trey said, when they were beside the springs that gave the place its name, the water of the flowing pool musical and dappled with starlight. "That's why I've got to tell you something I've never told anybody except for one judge, down in Colorado."

Rachel waited, barely able to breathe, her arms wrapped tightly around her middle.

He met her eyes. "My wife—Emma's mother—was killed when a couple of outlaws robbed a store in Great Falls," he said. She saw the memory of that day in his face, and grieved with him and for him, but she did not speak.

He thrust out a sigh. "I shot them, Rachel," he said. "One between the eyes, one through the heart."

Rachel swallowed. "In cold blood?" she whispered. She had no real sympathy for the dead outlaws; they were killers, after all, and thieves. But neither did she believe in taking the law into one's own hands.

"I didn't ambush them, if that's what you mean. Legally, I suppose, it was a fair fight. But yes, my blood was cold when I did it."

"Are you wanted?"

He considered the question. "No," he said. "I turned myself in to a marshal, down Colorado way, in a fit of good conscience. He refused to press charges and that was the end of it, as far as the law was concerned."

She just stood there, at a loss for what to say. Right or wrong, she loved him, and it wasn't her place to sit in judgment of what he'd done. She might, in fact, have done the same thing, in his place. "Then it's over," she said softly.

He took a step toward her, then stopped, plainly uncertain. "You've got to understand, Rachel," he said. "I'm not sorry for what I did. I'd do it again."

She bit her lower lip. "Fair enough," she said.

There was a long silence. Then he favored her with a tentative, lopsided grin. "If that's the way of it, Miss English, I'm through biding my time. I want to know what I have to do to make you my wife."

Rachel stared at him, her heart soaring. Although she'd been certain of her own feelings, she had, of course, not been entirely sure of his. "You want to marry me?"

Trey cleared his throat. He was holding his hat in both hands, turning it slowly between his fingers. "Yes," he said, after a long time. "I love you, Rachel. I wouldn't have chosen to, but I do."

Rachel wanted to fling her arms around his neck in pure jubilation, but she held herself back. There were too many things still unsettled. "I can't give up teaching," she said, after a very long time. "I won't."

Trey threw her own words back at her. "Fair enough," he said, with surprising readiness. "I don't mean to close down the saloon, so I guess we're even."

Rachel drew a deep breath, let it out slowly. "You must know it isn't a proper place to raise Emma or any other children who might come along," she said, in a nervous rush of words.

"I'll build you a house, if that's what you want. Hell, I'll sell my homestead to Landry Kildare and take out a mortgage at the bank over in Choteau.

Send for one of those mail-order places like Miss June-bug's always talking about, with the bathtubs and the hot water and all."

Rachel laid a hand to her heart. "You'd do that?"

"I told you," Trey said gravely. "I love you. Besides that, Teacher, if I can't bed you pretty damn soon, I'm going to have to start spending half my time sitting in the horse trough."

She laughed at the image, though his declaration had brought tears to her eyes. "There was someone else," she reminded him. "His name was Langdon and we were in love . . . we thought . . . we—"

He laid a finger to her lips. "That's past. All it means is that our wedding night will be a bit easier for you. Besides, Rachel, I'm not exactly pure myself, you know. There was Emma's mother, for one."

She swallowed. "I'll marry you, then, Trey Hargreaves. I'll raise your daughter as my own, and I'll bear your children, as many as you give me. I'll even live above that dratted saloon of yours—but only until our house is finished."

He pulled her close, grinning, and arranged her head for his impending kiss, the kiss that would seal their bargain. "Deal," he said, and brought his mouth down on hers.

The wedding was held a month later, by which time Trey had put in the order for a small house, which would be sent west from Chicago by rail and then freight wagon, to be erected on a plot of land well down the road from the Brimstone. School would start in just two weeks, and so far, no one had objected to having a married teacher in the school-house, so classes were to begin on schedule.

Folks came from all over to attend the ceremony, everyone from Granny Johnson to the Wainwright family. Evangeline had agreed to stand up for Rachel; Jacob would perform the service itself, of course, and June-bug was to sing.

Because it was a beautiful day, full summer now, the marriage party assembled in the grassy sideyard of the station, where tables had been set out and ribbons hung from the trees. Rachel wore June-bug's wedding dress, a lovely confection of ivory satin, dripping with lace, while Trey, looking nervous as an unshod horse on rocky ground, donned his dark suit.

Christabel and Emma had erected a bower of sorts, using wildflowers and foliage gathered in their wander-ings, under which Jacob would stand, facing the bride and groom.

June-bug's song had all the women in tears right off, Rachel included. Trey tugged at his shirt collar with one finger, obviously wishing the whole thing were over and done with. It would be a long time before he got his wish, though, because after the ceremony there was a community meal, everything from roast beef to wedding cake, and after that was another dance. While Rachel was equally anxious that they be alone together, it was after all her wedding day, the only one she ever intended to have, and she meant to savor every moment, be fully present for every joy. The pleasures of the night to come would take care of themselves.

The exchange of vows was relatively short, and within a few minutes, Jacob had pronounced Trey and Rachel to be man and wife. Trey turned to Rachel, wrapped both arms around her, and lifted her clear off her feet for his kiss. Hurrahs went up all around.

The meal followed—Rachel, now Mrs. Hargreaves, nibbled at a few things, but she had no real appetite. Trey, on the other hand, seemed ravenous, and consumed a plateful of fried chicken, sliced beef, deviled eggs, potato salad, and pickles. After that, he had cake, and while the women presented Rachel with intricately stitched quilt blocks cut from flour sacks and other yard goods, Trey hung his jacket on a tree limb, pushed up his sleeves, and proceeded to beat every man present at a game of horseshoes.

Rachel tried not to watch her new husband, but her gaze kept straying off in search of him, and she supposed her longing showed as plainly as her love. Although she was hardly experienced, she was no shrinking maiden either, and she anticipated the consummation of their marriage as much as Trey did.

The afternoon seemed endless, the hot, slow hours rolling by like whole days, but at last the evening came, and there was more food, and paper lanterns suspended among the ribbons, from the tree branches, were lit. Old Mr. Prudham produced his fiddle again, and the dancing began.

The first dance was, of course, a waltz, and Rachel and Trey moved together, into each other's arms, slowly whirling round and round beneath a summer moon. The grass smelled sweetly and Rachel's heart was full.

"You are very beautiful, Teacher," Trey said softly, looking down into her eyes. They were dancing alone, for this was the wedding waltz, reserved for the bride and groom. "I can't wait to have you to myself."

A sweet shiver went through Rachel, and she batted her eyelashes, pretending to be coy. "Why, Mr. Hargreaves, are you making improper advances?"

"Oh, yes, Mrs. Hargreaves," he answered. "Most improper." He kissed her lightly, quickly on the mouth. "I mean to have you carrying on something awful, and right soon now."

Rachel trembled; he felt it and smiled again.

"You have a lot of confidence in your abilities as a lover," she teased.

"All of it justified," Trey boasted shamelessly, "as you shall soon learn. Though not soon enough, I'm afraid, to suit your long-suffering husband."

She laughed. "Poor darling," she said, and stroked his smoothly shaven cheek with the back of one hand, "how will I comfort you?"

He made a growling sound and spun her around once, off her feet, before resuming the waltz. The wedding guests, hearing nothing but probably suspecting a great deal, laughed and applauded.

In time, as all things do, the wedding dance ended. Those visitors who weren't passing the night at the station, as the Wainwrights were, offered their last congratulations of the day and departed in wagons and buggies, on horseback and even on foot. Emma, plainly pleased to have Rachel for a stepmother as well as a teacher, was to board with the McCaffreys for a while, so the newlyweds would have the rooms over the saloon to themselves.

They walked through the sultry darkness together, Trey and Rachel, her hand clasped firmly in his. When they reached the bottom of the rear stairs, he suddenly swept her up into his arms and carried her. Reaching the door, he pushed it open with one foot, and then they were inside.

Rachel, who had been so cavalier before, was suddenly nervous. Teasing Trey at the party had been one thing, being alone with him in a darkened room, where they would soon make love for the first time, was quite another. Her heart began to race with a strange combination of anticipation and pure terror.

Trey kissed her, so deeply and so thoroughly that she stumbled when he set her on her feet and might have fallen if she hadn't reached out and grasped hold of something that turned out to be a bedpost, when he struck a match to a lamp wick and she could see her surroundings.

She stared at the magnificent carved bed in amazement. She hadn't noticed it when she had last visited the Hargreaves home, that day she'd taken tea and cookies with Emma and Trey, but then, she hadn't been out of the general living area.

Trey apparently read her mind. Shedding his coat, he nodded toward the lovely piece of furniture. "Pretty grand, isn't it?" he said, with a flashing grin. "I had it sent over from Choteau, and if you don't think I had a devil of a time keeping you from hearing about it, you'd best think again."

Rachel felt the mattress with a tentative push of one hand and found it firm but very inviting. For a major piece of furniture to arrive at Springwater without her seeing or getting word of it was indeed a remarkable thing. The arrival of the stagecoach was an event, let alone that of a freight wagon. "It's . . . lovely."

Trey unfastened his collar and tossed it aside. "Not so lovely as you are," he said, and his voice sounded husky, masculine—hungry. He approached Rachel and, standing before her, slipped his fingers into her hair and let it down, disregarding the many pins that tinkled to the floor. He kissed her again, and the contact left her drunk with wanting, actually swaying on her feet. On some remote level of her mind, she was wondering if she really had made love with Langdon, or only imagined that she had, for this was something altogether different.

When the kiss was over, he ran his mouth lightly along the edge of Rachel's jaw, igniting a thousand achy little fires under her flesh. "Do you know when I fell in love with you?" he asked, in a gruff whisper.

"W-When?" Rachel managed. She was fairly crackling with sensation by then, and hardly able to keep from flinging herself at Trey like a wanton.

"When you poked your head out of that stage window, with that stupid feather on your hat bobbing in the wind, and inquired if I was an outlaw."

Rachel might have laughed, if she hadn't been in a

state of sweet agony. "I fell in love with you," she said, "when you pulled me out of the coach and up onto your horse."

He nibbled at her mouth again, fairly driving her wild. "What took us so long to get from then to now?" he asked, unbuttoning the bodice of her borrowed dress, smoothing away the lovely old fabric, revealing her camisole and petticoat. He put his palms over her breasts, holding them gently but at the same time claiming them, and Rachel moaned as her nipples pressed themselves against him.

"Don't make me wait," she pleaded.

He lowered his suspenders, unbuttoned his shirt, took it off, and tossed it aside, all with maddening slowness. "I won't," he said, "not the first time, anyway. I don't have that kind of patience."

Rachel laid her hands to his chest, fingers splayed, and gloried in the feel of his warm, muscular flesh, the mat of dark hair, the hardening of his nipples. While they were kissing, he unlaced her camisole, baring her breasts, and fondled them until Rachel was half frantic to be taken.

Trey finished undressing her, then undressed himself, and eased her backward, onto the new bed, shipped all the way from Choteau. Onto the bed where their children would be conceived and born, where they themselves would die, one and then the other, when they were very, very old.

He stretched out beside her, took long, leisurely suckle at her breasts, and then moved over her, keeping most of his weight suspended on his forearms and elbows. She could see him plainly in the lamp-light, though it was dim, see the love and the passion in his eyes, and the question.

She nodded, and he parted her legs gently, with a motion of one knee. She felt him at the entrance to her body, hard and impossibly large, and for a moment her eyes widened and she was afraid.

He paused, waited.

Rachel nodded again, and he was inside her, in a single deep, smooth thrust; she felt herself expand to accommodate him, felt the breath flee her lungs as she was swept up on a wave of desire so high, so hot, so intense that her reason was left behind, spinning in a tidepool.

She cried his name, and scraped his back with her fingernails, and he moved faster, and deeper, ever deeper, until they were both on fire. Then, in a long, undulating flash, the world ended in a cataclysm of fire and light and ferocious pleasure that had them both shouting in release.

When it was over, and their bodies were still at last, and spent, Trey fell beside Rachel, gasping and holding her tightly against his chest. They were both damp with exertion, and she could feel his heart pounding beneath her cheek.

"If I'd known just how good that was going to be," he said, when he found his breath, "I believe I would have been scared."

Rachel laughed, though her eyes were brimming with tears—tears of homecoming, of joy, of restored hope. "I thought I was dying," she said, in all honesty. "I couldn't see, I couldn't hear or think—all I could do was feel."

He rolled onto his side and kissed her, very lightly, but with the promise of much more. "Give me a few minutes," he said, "and I'll take you back up there, to the other side of the stars."

She stretched, wondering when her melted limbs would be solid again. "Maybe we'd better wait a little while," she suggested, "just until all my pulses settle down."

He bent his head, took her nipple in his mouth and drew it into a primal dance with the tip of his tongue, causing her to moan and arch her back slightly. "Not a chance," he said, after long moments of brazen enjoyment. "Tonight, you're the student, and *I'm* the teacher, and the lessons have only begun."

Rachel whimpered. She felt as though she'd just been hurled to the top of a mountain and then sent careening down again, and she was still wobbly at the knees. Now he was telling her that there were still more sweeping pleasures ahead. "Suppose I can't bear it?" she fretted.

He found the hollow of her throat and nibbled there. "Oh, you can bear it, all right," he promised, and proceeded to prove it. And prove it. And prove it again. By the time they finally slept, well toward morning, Rachel was exhausted, but she dreamed. She dreamed of silver-eyed babies and a mail-order house with a white picket fence out front and flowers growing in the yard. She dreamed of Emma, grown and beautiful, wearing a wedding dress of her own, and of a busy, thriving town, and a brick schoolhouse, and a white church with a belltower.

In Trey's arms, in his bed, it was so easy to dream.

Rachel was nervous the day school started; her pupils watched her with mischievous eyes and whispered behind their hands when they thought she wasn't looking. She couldn't imagine what they were discussing, and wasn't sure she wanted to know, but order had to be restored.

She clapped her hands together twice, and sharply. "That will be enough giggling and talking!" she said, in her best schoolmarm tones.

Marcus Kildare waved one hand in the air, and Rachel called on him to speak, even though she knew he was up to something. "Emma says she's going to get a baby brother or sister soon. Is that true?"

Emma folded her arms and lifted her chin, her eyes bright with certainty.

Rachel felt color flood her face, but she did not allow her shoulders to droop, nor did she avert her gaze. As it happened, she suspected that she was already in the family way, but she had told no one but Trey and June-bug. The physical part of her marriage was intense, but Emma couldn't have known that, since she was staying with the McCaffreys until the mail-order house arrived and was set up.

"Mr. Hargreaves and I hope to have a child soon, yes."

Emma looked vindicated. She turned to Marcus Kildare and put out her tongue. He responded in kind.

"Enough," Rachel said. "We are here to learn." With that, she began her first day of classes. When school let out at three o'clock, she made a point of not hurrying across the street and around to the rear door of the Brimstone Saloon, lest that raise undue speculation.

Trey was standing at the stove when she came in, sipping coffee, and he'd already turned the bedclothes back. "Hello, Mrs. Hargreaves," he said. "How was your day?"

Rachel closed the door and lowered the latch. "Long," she answered, but she wasn't the least bit tired and they both knew it. She started to undress, but Trey crossed the room and stopped her, taking both her wrists in his hands and bending his head to kiss her. It was a ravenous exchange, no tamer on Rachel's part than his.

"Just let me get out of these clothes," she murmured, barely able to speak, when he withdrew his mouth.

"No," he said, and raised her skirts to unfasten her drawers and peel them down over her hips. She stepped out of them, never looking away from his eyes, and he sat down and drew her with him, causing her to sit astraddle of him. She flung back her head in an agony of exultation when he unfastened his trousers and then entered her, filled her.

He opened her bodice then, to tongue and suckle

her breasts, all the while raising and lowering her along the length of him, his hands firm and strong on her hips. They climaxed together, and Rachel fell forward, to let her head rest against his shoulder. She could still feel him pulsing within her.

"How long can we keep this up?" she asked, when she could manage even those simple words.

"Oh," he drawled, "for a long, long time, Mrs. Hargreaves. Maybe forever." With that, he stood, carried her to the bed, and made love to her again, even more thoroughly than before, and far more slowly.

Neither of them heard the stagecoach thundering into town, right on schedule, the driver shouting, the hooves of the horses pounding on the hard ground, the wheels squeaking as if all the demons of hell were in close pursuit. They had other concerns, Mr. and Mrs. Trey Hargreaves, and for them, the outside world was a very distant place.

Linda Lael Miller

SPRINGWATER SEASONS

Rachel

Savannah

Miranda

Jessica

The breathtaking new series....Discover the passion,
the pride, and the glory of a magnificent frontier town!

Coming soon from Pocket Books   2043

LINDA LAEL MILLER

TWO BROTHERS
THE GUNSLINGER
THE LAWMAN

"Linda Lael Miller's talent knows no bounds...each story she creates is...superb."
—*Rendezvous*

**Available now
from Pocket Books**

2009-01

LINDA LAEL MILLER